SIX O'CLOCK SILENCE

Also by Joanne Pence

The Ancient Secrets Novels
ANCIENT ECHOES
ANCIENT SHADOWS
ANCIENT ILLUSIONS

The Rebecca Mayfield Mysteries
ONE O'CLOCK HUSTLE
TWO O'CLOCK HEIST
THREE O'CLOCK SÉANCE
FOUR O'CLOCK SIZZLE
FIVE O'CLOCK TWIST
SIX O'CLOCK SILENCE
THE THIRTEENTH SANTA (Novella)

The Angie & Friends Food & Spirits Mysteries
COOKING SPIRITS
ADD A PINCH OF MURDER
COOK'S BIG DAY
MURDER BY DEVIL'S FOOD
COOK'S CURIOUS CHRISTMAS (A Fantasy EXTRA)

Other Novels
DANCE WITH A GUNFIGHTER
THE DRAGON'S LADY
SEEMS LIKE OLD TIMES
THE GHOST OF SQUIRE HOUSE
DANGEROUS JOURNEY

SIX O'CLOCK SILENCE

AN INSPECTOR REBECCA MAYFIELD MYSTERY

JOANNE PENCE

QUAIL HILL PUBLISHING

This is a work of fiction. Names, characters, places, public or private institutions, corporations, towns, and incidents are the product of the author's imagination or are used fictitiously. Any resemblance to actual events, locales, or persons, living or dead, is coincidental.

No part of this book may be reproduced or transmitted in any form or by any electronic or mechanical means including information storage and retrieval systems without permission in writing from the author, except by a reviewer who may quote brief passages in a review. This book may not be resold or uploaded for distribution to others.

Quail Hill Publishing

PO Box 64

Eagle, ID 83616

Visit our website at www.quailhillpublishing.net

First Quail Hill Publishing E-book: January 2018

First Quail Hill Print Book: January 2018

Second Quail Hill Print Book: August 2018

Copyright (c) 2018 Joanne Pence
All rights reserved.
ISBN: 978-0998245959

SIX O'CLOCK SILENCE

1

As I drive through quiet, fog-laden streets of the city, I'm filled with memories of all you once meant to me and how it all turned out so wrong.

I warned you. I taught you to fear. And ironically, it was me you came to fear. You couldn't see the real me. All you saw was your idea of me. All you heard were my words of warning, but not what was in my heart.

You were wrong. But I, too, was wrong to push you away. You and I never should have happened, but you sneaked up on me, wormed your way into my life, into my heart, with your goodness.

Yet, you weren't all that good, were you? If you were, you never would have cheated on the man you married. You didn't love him, that was clear. You loved him once, or so you claimed, but as the years passed, you grew into a dull acceptance of life, of boredom.

When we met, you said you had never known anyone like me. That I fascinated you with my silences, my strange life, and that I inflicted death on others with what you believed to be ease, and what I knew to be justice.

You said you loved me, but more than that, you feared me—feared me not for what I was, but for all I had come to mean to you.

I could not fight your fear.

In the end, I sent you back to the life you despised. And you hated me for it.

I vowed I would never contact you again, and made you promise me the same, even while knowing that together we were more than either of us is apart.

I ignored your tears as I walked away, and I didn't look back.

I have always been a man of my word.

2

Four days earlier—

San Francisco Homicide Inspector Rebecca Mayfield and her partner, Homicide Inspector Bill Sutter, stood at the edge of a trench dug to lay sewer lines in the far western portion of Golden Gate Park. The area, up to this time untouched by most park users, consisted of pine and fir trees, shrubs, a rarely visited old Dutch windmill, and a small tulip garden. But as the city's population grew, the Recreation and Park Commission decided to install public restrooms to prepare for future activity centers. The sewer lines would connect the restroom to the city system.

The trench was the length of two football fields, and deep. Along it were mounds of dirt that had been excavated.

As best Rebecca and Sutter could determine, none of the workmen had noticed anything unusual about the site until they arrived that morning. They found that something—most likely dogs or foxes—had dug through some of the dirt and scattered a number of small bones and one large one. The foreman believed the bones were human and called the police.

"I'd say the foreman is right," Rebecca said. Thirty-five years of age, she was tall, with large blue eyes in a triangular face ending in a pointed chin. Her straight blond hair was pulled back in a ponytail. "The bones look as if they're from a human hand, as in fingers. And the longer one could be a forearm."

The bones weren't the clean white color seen in museums or medical schools, but were a deep, mottled brown. All had been gnawed on, their ends ragged. But until someone with medical and forensic knowledge studied them, no one currently at the crime scene could officially state what they were looking at.

"I suspect," Sutter said, pointing at the undisturbed land on either side of the trench, "the rest of the body must be in there somewhere." Sutter was in his fifties, with short gray hair and a wiry build. He consistently spent more time planning for his retirement than thinking about his cases, but somehow couldn't bring himself to turn in the "I'm-outta-here" paperwork.

"If someone buried an entire body out here," Rebecca said, "whoever did it picked one of the least busy areas of San Francisco. If those new sewer pipes weren't being installed, the site might have gone on undisturbed for quite a few more years."

"I always thought only vagrants and people wanting to hide from prying eyes come to this part of the park," Sutter said. "Seems like a waste of taxpayer money building restrooms way out here. No one, least of all me, ever expected this new construction."

Rebecca ignored most of the comment, but Sutter did have a point. "Which means, whoever buried the body—or parts of the body—here, must have assumed it would remain well hidden. That it would never be discovered. It also means it's highly likely our corpse's death was no accident."

She walked away from the trench, Sutter following. "Let's get these bones packed up and to the lab and shut this site down until we have a better idea of what's going on out here."

Richie Amalfi turned his Porsche northward, across the Golden Gate Bridge to the town of Terra Linda, a place filled with 1950's Eichler homes that apparently were once the be-all and end-all of modern suburban living. These were now a bit of a curiosity, as in people being curious over what the public ever saw in them.

He parked in front of the home of Brian Skarzer, shut off the engine, and wondered for the hundredth time if he was being very, very stupid. Skarzer was the branch manager of Superior Savings Bank where Richie's fiancée, Isabella Russo, had been working at the time of her death, four years earlier.

Richie still had a few questions about what had happened back then, and he expected Skarzer had some answers.

He had tried for years to ignore his uneasiness over the accident that took Isabella's life, telling himself he was being paranoid, and unwilling to accept that horrible things do happen to many good people. But then, a few weeks back, Richie became entangled in one of Rebecca's cases that involved an old real estate friend of his, Audrey Poole.

In the course of running down a scheme involving phony international transactions, Audrey told Richie that Superior Savings Bank held the account for "Audrey Poole Investment Holdings," aka "API Holdings." Her words implied someone at the bank knew Audrey had been playing fast and loose with real estate laws.

Not long after talking to Richie, Audrey had been murdered —a murder that Rebecca had solved.

Since Isabella's job was as a loan officer, Richie couldn't help but think she might have looked closely at the way API Holdings handled the real estate transactions. If so, he wondered if she found something criminal which, given

Audrey's company, wouldn't have been difficult to do. And what if someone involved had decided to silence Isabella?

Richie had spent the past month looking into the bank with his friend, Henry Ian Tate III, aka "Shay." They didn't like what they saw. Four men had sufficient access to the bank's records to know what actions taken by API Holdings were illegal, and to keep those activities hidden from bank auditors. The four were Brian Skarzer, the branch manager; Grant Yamada, the assistant branch manager; Ethan Nolan, the senior data operations manager; and Isabella's assistant loan officer, Cory Egerton. Three of them still worked at the bank. Cory Egerton had left soon after Isabella's death, and so far, neither Richie or Shay could track him down.

Richie steeled himself. Time to act. He needed to talk to those men, to see how they reacted to him and to any hint that foul play had resulted in Isabella's death. He got out of the car and rang the bell.

A teenage boy came to the door. "Who are you?" The kid's lips contorted with derision.

"I'm looking for Brian Skarzer," Richie replied.

"If you're selling something or want to convert him, he's not interested." The obnoxious teen started to shut the door in Richie's face.

He put his foot next to the door jamb. "Do many Jehovah's Witnesses come to see you driving a Porsche?"

The kid angled his head to check the street. "That's yours?"

Richie nodded.

"Just a minute."

Richie saw a man, probably in his mid-fifties, medium height, pudgy, with a comb-over that didn't succeed in hiding the glare from his bald spot approach the open door. "You're here to see me?" he asked.

"I want to talk to you about Isabella Russo," Richie said.

Skarzer looked momentarily puzzled. "Why? You with the police or something?"

"Several questions have come up in the course of reviewing some insurance payments made at the time," Richie said. "I've been asked to look into them. The name is Richard Doolittle. I'm with a private firm. We hope to resolve our issues quietly with no police involvement."

Skarzer turned skeptical. "Insurance questions? After how many years? Four? Five?" Since Richie remained impassively at the door staring at him, Skarzer scowled. "Well, I guess you may as well come in."

He led Richie into a small living room with a large TV. His wife came out of the kitchen. Skarzer introduced Lois to Richie and made it clear this was a "work" visit and she needed to leave. She did.

"Now," Skarzer said when they were seated and alone in the room, "what can I do for you?"

"We're looking into some occurrences that took place around the time Ms. Russo was killed," Richie said. "One of the things that stood out was that her assistant, Cory Egerton, left your employ just a few months after her death, and now, it seems no one knows where he's located."

"What in the world does Cory Egerton have to do with an insurance claim on Isabella?" Skarzer asked.

"Please, just answer the question." It was all Richie could do not to wipe the sneer off the guy's face.

"Well, you said no one knows where he is, and I guess I'm among them." Skarzer sounded annoyed. "It's not as if I keep track of my former employees."

Richie gritted his teeth. "Maybe you can tell me something about Egerton. What was his relationship to Ms. Russo?"

"He was her assistant. Beyond that, I have no idea."

"Think about it." Richie's eyes narrowed with a clear message not to even attempt to challenge him.

"You look somewhat familiar to me," Skarzer said, pushing back. "Why is that?"

Richie shrugged. "I've been in your bank a few times."

A look of sudden recognition flashed across Skarzer's face. "I remember now. You were engaged to her. You used to come by the bank all the time." His gaze hardened. "You can get out of my house."

"I've just got a few questions, and then I'll be on my way." Richie's tone was mild, reasonable, even as he made no attempt to move.

Skarzer grimaced, staring hard at him. "Why are you really here?"

"As I said, I've still got some questions about her death."

"After all this time?"

"What the hell does time matter when there are too many unanswered questions, such as why Egerton left the bank so soon afterward."

Skarzer grimaced and strode to built-in shelves, where a small bar-like setup stood among books and knickknacks. He poured himself about three-fingers of bourbon. He drank down half of it and didn't offer any to Richie. "The guy was disappointed that he didn't get Isabella's position after she passed away. That's all. He was clever, extremely clever, with the technical side of the work. He understood our computer programs inside and out, but he had no people skills. The last thing we wanted was him as a team leader."

"Can you think of anyone who might know where he's gone?"

Skarzer sat again, still gripping the bourbon-filled glass. "No. You might check with Personnel. They probably sent him paperwork. Also, many people who have worked for us keep their accounts open since we offer good rates to current and past employees."

"Okay, thanks." Richie stood, as if to leave. "One last question. It appears Isabella was coming here—to your home—to see you the morning she was killed. Could you tell me the reason for such an early visit?"

"That's completely wrong. She wasn't coming to see me." Skarzer appeared sincerely shocked by the suggestion. "I have no idea where she was going. Frankly, we rarely spoke when she was at work, so I find it hard to imagine she'd be coming to my home at any hour of the day, let alone such an early one."

Richie nodded. He had to admit, he believed Skarzer—Isabella wouldn't have wasted her time talking to such a schmuck.

He wouldn't waste any more time talking to the schmuck either.

3

That evening, Rebecca parked her older black Ford Explorer atop a red "no parking" zone in the dead-end street where her apartment was located. Richie's nearly new Porsche 911 Turbo sat a couple of doors away, also in a red zone. Fortunately, meter maids giving out parking tickets never bothered to drive into tiny Mulford Alley.

When Rebecca first moved to San Francisco, she received a sticker that allowed her to park for free in her own neighborhood. What it didn't say was that very few such "free" parking spots existed. In fact, she almost never found one open. After a couple of weeks, she realized if she didn't park illegally, her only option was a pay lot, and they were beyond expensive in the busy part of town—between Nob Hill and the Tenderloin—where Rebecca lived.

She found Richie in her apartment. Just seeing him made her heart beat a little faster and her evening a little brighter. He was only a little taller than her five-feet ten-inches, with deep-set, dark eyes, prominent cheekbones, and a Roman, aquiline nose. His clothes were always expensive and stylish, and he wore his wavy black hair slightly long and expertly trimmed. He was, in a word, handsome.

The TV was on, and delicious smells came from the tiny kitchen. Not only the kitchen was tiny, the entire apartment was. The building consisted of two large upper flats, and a garage that took up most of the ground floor. Her apartment, such as it was, had once been a storeroom in the back of that garage. Converted to a two-room living space that opened to the backyard, it now held a combination living-dining-kitchen, plus a bedroom with a bathroom so small it made airplane johns seem spacious. The furniture, like the apartment itself, was old and mismatched, but comfortable.

Of course, the city's building code considered such an apartment completely illegal. The irony of her being a cop and living and parking illegally was not lost on her.

Her little residence was a far cry from Richie's spacious home atop Twin Peaks with a beautiful view of the city and bay. Still, he seemed to enjoy visiting her and her little Chihuahua-Chinese Crested hairless mix named Spike, and she came to accept the fact that she didn't mind him dropping in uninvited, and that she missed him when he wasn't there.

She especially didn't mind the visits when he brought her something good to eat.

She breathed in the aromatic scent. "What smells so good?" she asked as she took off her jacket.

"Hello to you, too," he said as he peeked in the oven. "And I'm happy to see you."

"Uh, oh, Spike," she said, patting Spike's head in greeting. "Now he's insulted." She faced Richie. "Hello. How *ever* are you? And what smells so delicious?"

Richie grinned.

She liked his smile, liked everything about him, truth be told.

"It's Carmela's lasagna. She brought over a casserole for me.

It's more than enough for two, but I'd never tell her that." He picked up an unlabeled wine bottle from the kitchen counter. "And here's some of my Uncle Sil's vino. The best."

"It sounds heavenly." She took off her gun and holster, then kept her gaze glued to his as she walked toward him. He put down the wine bottle, one eyebrow raised, as she slid her arms around his neck. "And since Carmela brought the lasagna to you, I know it hasn't been poisoned."

Despite the fact that Carmela's only son was nearly forty years old and had never been married, Carmela watched over him like a mother bear guarding her cub. Rebecca had gotten between the two of them at her peril. Not only was Rebecca not Italian, and not Catholic, she was a cop, which meant—in Carmela's mind—that she often put Richie in danger. Little did Carmela know how much danger Richie put himself into, danger that Rebecca usually had nothing to do with, and often warned him against.

"Carmela loves you." Richie smiled as his arms circled her, drawing her close.

She kissed him. "Sure she does."

He kissed her back. "She told me so. How can I not believe my own mother?" Her heartbeat quickened at his touch, her arms tightened, wanting him closer, much closer, but then, abruptly, he pulled away. "Listen, I found this thumbtacked on your door." Surprised, she let him go as he took a piece of paper from his pocket. "It's got me worried."

He handed it to her. It was a picture of a skull and crossbones—a sign of poison or a pirate ship. "Do you know why it's there?"

She carefully looked over the front and back of the small sheet. "No, but I found the same drawing under my car's windshield wipers at work today."

"*What?*" Richie bellowed. "Someone is telling you he knows where you live and where you work. This means danger."

"Yeah, and I'm quaking in my boots." Her tone was sarcastic. "I face bullets. I face *you*. Some little pencil sketch isn't going to scare me."

"It's no joke. This should scare you! It's a warning."

Rebecca dropped the paper into a baggie. "I've pissed off a lot of people as a cop. I'm used to threats. But, for you, I'll give it to the CSI unit to look for fingerprints. Happy?"

He didn't look happy, but turned away to take the casserole out of the oven. "The lasagna is hot. It needs to sit a few minutes."

Rebecca put together a salad while Richie sliced some sourdough bread. Then he opened the wine and poured them each a glass.

Rebecca watched him work in silence.

Silence ... that wasn't like him. In fact, given the way she'd greeted him, she was surprised they weren't in her bedroom right now. Something was definitely wrong.

"*Salut*," both said as their glasses clinked. His dark eyes followed her. But then she turned and walked to the dining table. Still, he said nothing. Richie was usually the more animated one, talkative and joking.

"You're quiet tonight." She studied him as they both sat.

"Am I?"

"You aren't mad because I'm not all freaked out about a skull and crossbones, are you? Believe me, if anyone dressed up as a pirate comes after me, I'll know I should have listened to you."

"Very funny. But you're right—I may be over-reacting." He took a big bite of lasagna and then a sip of wine.

She, too, began to eat, but couldn't help studying him and wondering for the umpteenth time how he managed to become such a big part of her life. Tonight he seemed different, though, almost sad. His deep-set dark eyes were downcast. She took in the faint lines along their outer edges—"crow's feet" she'd heard them called. And few gray hairs punctuated the temples of his thick, wavy black hair. She reached out and placed her hand on his.

"Is something wrong?" she asked.

"I'm just a little tired. It's nothing." His words were soft, introspective, but then he said, "Tell me about your day."

As they polished off more than half of Carmela's lasagna, which Rebecca found to be the best she had ever tasted, she told Richie about the ugly meeting that took place that very morning with her boss, Lt. Eastwood. "He called me into his office and told me the mayor wasn't happy with my performance in Homicide. The mayor, mind you, as if he knows anything about the cases I've worked over the years."

"Why did he say that?" Richie asked.

"Because I questioned the mayor's chief-of-staff about a case."

"Oh yes, your old boyfriend."

"Sean Hinkle wasn't a boyfriend. I only dated him a few times. But anyway, the mayor believes I 'badgered' Sean, which led to his suicide. Is that ridiculous or what? Frankly, I never believed that Sean killed himself, but it wasn't my case."

Richie let out a low whistle. "That's a good reason for the mayor to be irritated."

She put down her fork. "Don't you dare say that! I had nothing to do with Sean's death. I tried to defend myself to Eastwood, but he wouldn't hear it. He sided with the mayor. And if you do, too—"

"Calm down." Richie held up his hands in an 'I surrender' gesture. "I know you acted correctly. And I think your boss is a real shithead."

She smiled even as she took a deep breath. "Good. And yes, he is. I keep hoping he'll get promoted out of Homicide. That might be the only way I'll be free of him."

"Yeah, except that he's already beyond the Peter Principle."

She thought a moment. "That's where you keep getting promoted until you reach a point where you're incompetent, and then you're stuck in that position forever, right?"

"You got it."

"That's not encouraging, Richie." She frowned. "It would mean my career has ended as well. No way will Eastwood ever recommend me for promotion."

"Don't worry," he said softly. "People know how good you are. You'll be running the place long before Eastwood. And then you can fire him."

She lifted her wine glass. "I'll drink to that."

"Me, too."

Dinner over, as the two cleaned up the kitchen and Richie still wasn't being his usual talkative self, something came to mind that would surely intrigue him, and possibly get him out of his funk. "Eastwood did one good thing today," Rebecca said. "He sent Sutter and me to a case that may turn out more interesting than he ever expected. Some workmen found a few bones in Golden Gate Park. I suspect Eastwood thought the bones were some animal's. But this afternoon, the Medical Examiner confirmed that they're human. We've now got the crime scene unit out there looking for the rest of the body."

"The rest of the body?" he repeated. "That doesn't sound good."

"No, it's not. We saw no flesh, just bones—a hand and forearm. It seemed they'd been buried for some time."

"Buried like in a grave?"

"Possibly. Some pipe layers were out there digging a deep trench for a new sewer line." While Rebecca covered the remaining lasagna and refrigerated it, Richie filled the dishwasher.

"What if," Richie shuddered, "they've stumbled across an old Indian burial ground? That's not good mojo, you know."

"Hopefully, it's nothing like that."

They moved into the living room and sat on the sofa. She studied him. "Are you sure there's nothing wrong?"

"Why?"

Because you're letting me do most of the talking. She always enjoyed Richie's ability to talk about anything, anytime, and to simply be entertaining in an often humdrum world. But tonight, he was unnaturally quiet. Finally, she said, "You seem to have something on your mind."

"Not at all. How about a movie?" he asked.

"I'd probably fall asleep." She gave him a smile and come-hither lift of her eyebrows. That type of comment always led him to some sort of suggestive remark. She felt rather suggestive herself tonight. She waited.

"Oh."

That's all? She put her hand on his knee. "There are better ways to spend an evening."

"You're sleepy," he said and stood up. "I'd better get going and let you get some rest."

She was stunned.

He wore a strange expression as he gently touched the side of her face. "Yeah, that would be best." He picked up his jacket and patted Spike.

"I'll call soon," he said, and then left the apartment.

She stared at the door he had just exited without giving her a goodnight kiss or even a backward glance. She was certain something was very wrong indeed.

4

Richie rested his head against the high back of his leather chair. It was early afternoon, and he was in the office of his nightclub, Big Caesar's. He had never imagined he would become a nightclub owner, but when a deadbeat owed him a lot of money and couldn't pay cash, he gave Richie the club instead. The club had been losing money at the time, but now, despite everyone warning him that nightclub ownership was a fool's mission and a great way to lose one's shirt, the club was doing quite well.

At this hour, Big Caesar's was empty. Richie liked being there with no one else around. He used the quiet time to go over his books and to figure out which bands, singers, and types of music made money and which didn't. He had a bookkeeper and an accountant, but he'd learned long ago that the easiest way to fail at a business was to rely on other people's advice on how to run it.

He sat at his desk, a beautiful walnut desk in an elegantly remodeled office that even had its own bathroom with a shower. No one who knew him as the scruffy little fatherless boy who spent most of his time on the streets would imagine such an office could one day be his.

But now, as he looked at the figures on a spreadsheet in front of him, he wasn't able to concentrate. The numbers might have been chicken scratchings for all the sense they made.

He felt bad—bad about asking Shay to look into Isabella's actions prior to her death, and bad about the way he'd walked out on Rebecca last night. Rebecca was warm, desirable, and caring—but after a day filled with memories of Isabella, he felt as if being with Rebecca was some kind of insult to Isabella's memory—as if he were being unfaithful to her.

Such a reaction was wrong, and he knew it. Stupid. Childish. Assholish—if there was such a word. He called himself every name in the book, but he simply hadn't learned to compartmentalize his life the way some people could. "Then" versus "now." That wasn't him. His life was one big emotional jumble. And sometimes he hated himself for it.

He rubbed the skin under his eyes and tried once more to concentrate on the financial reports before him.

But his wayward thoughts only delved deeper into the troubling situation.

He would never forget the day he walked into Superior Savings Bank, and his life changed forever.

Isabella Russo was a bank loan officer. On that particular day, a stomach flu had spread through the teller staff, so it was "all hands on deck" to help customers. Since Richie's usual teller was out sick, he had sauntered over to the woman with rakishly short black hair who stood in her place. Her dark eyes were heavy with mascara that made her lashes the longest he'd ever seen, and her dark red lipstick matched the color of her dress.

"Where's Nancy?" he had asked. Nancy was *the* blonde bombshell of the bank. He always did his best to get into her line.

"She's sick today, Mr. Amalfi." Isabella gazed up at him through those maddening lashes, and a smile slowly crept across her face. The effect hit him like a bolt of lightning, leaving him almost at a loss for words. Almost.

He was initially surprised she knew his name, but since he did talk to and flirt with Nancy every week, he imagined word got around. "Oh, okay." He cleared his throat. "Well, I'd like to withdraw nine thousand nine hundred dollars."

"What size bills?"

"Hundreds."

"One moment."

He waited as she got the money, returned with nine thousand-dollar packets, and then counted out nine single C-notes. "Thanks," he said, gathering it all together.

"Mr. Amalfi, maybe I shouldn't say anything, but I'm wondering why you're taking out such an amount."

He noticed her left cheek formed a slight dimple as she spoke.

"It's not ten grand, so what's it to you?" He jutted out his chin.

"I know the Feds tell everyone they don't look at any withdrawals less than ten grand." With that, her dark brown eyes caught his and held steadily as she added, "But I normally work with loans and in accounting, and if you've *in any way* caught their attention ... Look up the definition of a crime called 'structuring'." She lifted an eyebrow.

Richie got the message. His mouth went dry as the implication of her words struck. And then, two things happened. He realized that he and everyone else who listened to the Feds were being played for fools. And that he was in love.

"May I ask you something?" he said.

"Sure."

"May I take you to lunch today?"

They were nearly inseparable after that.

Everyone liked her. Even his mother. What was not to like? Isabella Russo was Italian, Catholic, had never been married, wanted kids, and could make ravioli from scratch, a skill she had learned from her saintly, now departed, grandmother. Richie was in seventh heaven. His only problem was that she seemed so perfect, he constantly feared it would all blow up in his face. His friends, relatives, even his mother, Carmela, told him he was wrong. "Ask the girl to marry you, Richie," Carmela would say. "What do you think? She's gonna say 'No'? Are you that *pazzo?*"

No, he wasn't crazy.

He had thought about proposing for nearly a year, the whole time afraid to ask, afraid she'd turn him down, or that simply asking would turn karma against him.

He was scared. He admitted it. Nothing had ever been easy for him. From the time he was a kid, he had to fight for everything he ever wanted, for everything he ever achieved. Meeting and falling in love with Isabella seemed to have happened too easily. Other people met and married and lived charmed lives. But he didn't think that would ever happen to him. Then, finally, three years after meeting her, he proposed.

And she said yes.

He was the happiest man alive.

For three days.

But then...

Memories flooded over him, shaking him to the core.

But then she'd been killed in an inexplicable single car accident on the approach to the Golden Gate Bridge, a deadly roadway that long-time San Franciscans called "Doyle Drive," but had been officially re-named the "Presidio Parkway." No matter what its name, lots of bad accidents happened there. He always knew it was dangerous. So did Isabella.

What he didn't know, however, was why she was there at six o'clock in the morning, heading north, away from the city. He nearly went crazy from not knowing. Why was she there? Where was she going? If she was going to meet someone, who? Why? He never found any answers.

The evening before, she had called him and said she couldn't see him because something had come up at work, something big, and she needed to get all the facts straight before a meeting "with all the bosses" the following morning.

She had been putting in a lot of overtime, and something at the bank bothered her. He didn't worry about it. Why should he? How dangerous was working in a bank's loan department? Plus, she had no cash in her office and, in the rare situation of an armed robbery, her office was in the back, away from the tellers.

Not even her working late worried him. The bank's Marina district location was one of the safest areas of the city, and she lived less than five miles away on Telegraph Hill. In fact, she still lived with her parents, which made her affair with Richie a bit difficult, but at the same time, kind of old-fashioned and sweet—two things he had never experienced with any girlfriend before her. Fortunately, back then he was living in a condo he called his own, and she spent a lot of time there. He always made sure she reached home before her parents woke in the morning. That was their deal. And if her parents heard the key in the lock, or heard her tiptoeing up the stairs in the middle of the night, they had the good taste not to say anything. They weren't crazy about Richie when they first met him—like everyone else, they'd heard stories about him being "connected"—but they quickly realized he wasn't a lost cause, and had a lot of good in him. They suspected that Isabella was exactly what he needed to straighten out his errant ways and often told both of them so.

No one, not her friends, parents, or coworkers had any idea where she was going on that fateful morning. Several of the bank's bosses lived beyond the Golden Gate Bridge in Marin

County. But every one of them claimed to have been home asleep at that time of the morning, and none had been expecting a visit from their loan officer, or could imagine what couldn't wait until their morning meeting.

He didn't want to think there could be any connection between the illegal real estate dealings he'd recently learned about and Isabella's death, but what if there were? What would he do about it?

He knew what he wanted to do. Make the bastards pay. But how, without destroying his own life even more than he had already?

That wasn't fair. His life was hardly destroyed—although he would admit it seemed pretty damned fraught much of the time. Not that he cared. Or, he didn't *used to* care.

Now, things were changing. He could feel himself changing, feel himself drawn to the idea of leading a quieter life, one not so filled with messed-up people getting themselves into trouble and needing someone to "fix" the situation for them. Even—dare he think it?—to settle down with a good woman.

With Rebecca, if she'd have him, and if she'd give up running around the city after murderers.

The last thing he wanted, especially now, was to dredge up any of the old pain that had consumed him when his fiancée died. For Chrissakes, life is for the living. Yet, he had unanswered questions. Now, for the first time since Isabella's death, he had a small hint of where he might find some answers.

Just then, the buzzer by the back door sounded. A glance at the security screen showed who was out there: Shay. He buzzed the door open and in a short while, Shay walked into the office.

He was a tall man, taller than Richie, and while he seemed lithe, his body was rock-solid and muscular. Between his unique style of dress—that afternoon he wore a heather sports jacket, gray slacks, and a tan and green plaid ascot—and his wavy blond hair, blue eyes, and chiseled good looks, he always caught the eye of women. And held it ... until they got to know him.

He could be more than a little cold and intimidating, and that was on a good day. On a bad day, he could be downright scary. Plus, he was a military-trained sniper, and the best computer hacker Richie had ever known.

"Any luck?" Richie asked. He got up from his desk and moved to the liquor cabinet.

"Only bad." Shay sat on the sofa, facing Richie. "Something must have spooked whoever had been overseeing the bank accounts of API Holding because last night, they vanished."

"Vanished?"

"They're no longer on the bank's main system. The bad news is I'm going to have to find where the account's data is now. The good news is, once I find it, I should be able to track down who moved it. That could be a major clue as to who knew about the real estate holding company's illegal activities."

"My visit to the branch manager had to be the reason for the move. Either Skarzer moved the records, or he told someone about my visit and that person moved them. But we now know, of the four bankers possibly involved in the scheme, that Egerton is out since he no longer works at the bank, but one or more of the remaining three must definitely be involved."

"Involved with the holding company, yes, but not necessarily having anything to do with Isabella's accident," Shay reminded him.

Richie poured himself a straight shot of Stolichnaya and offered Shay a drink. Shay refused. Richie didn't drink much hard liquor and almost never in the afternoon, but thinking about Isabella always brought out the worst in him. He drank it down in one gulp. "True. Maybe you should just forget all this."

"I can," Shay said, unhappily eying Richie still holding the vodka bottle. "But can you?"

"Probably not." Richie put down the liquor and sat in a chair facing Shay.

Shay nodded. "That's what I thought. Have you told Rebecca you're looking into this?"

"Why should I?"

"You don't think she'll notice that there's something going on? You're not exactly taking this well, you know."

Richie rubbed his chin. "She kept asking me if there was something wrong last night. Instead of talking about it, I split. Part of me felt like I was copping out."

"Right, like that'll stop her from being curious about you," Shay said.

"At least she's got a new case. It's different. Hopefully, it'll distract her."

"Different?" Shay asked.

"Bones." Richie grimaced.

Shay couldn't help but smile at Richie's pained expression. "A skeleton?"

"Not exactly. Some workers found a hand and arm out in Golden Gate Park. Now, Rebecca wants to find the rest of the body."

"Golden Gate Park?" Shay said quizzically, then added, "With all the people around there, someone dumped some bones? It sounds like a prank."

"Apparently not. She said the city decided to put in some restrooms at the western edge of the park since more and more people are going out that way—*going* in all meanings of the word, apparently. Anyway, some guys were out there digging a trench for the sewer pipes, and dug up the bones. They were plenty deep, according to Rebecca."

"Oh," Shay murmured softly. "I see."

Richie chuckled. "I told her to beware of Indian burial grounds. She didn't take that well."

Shay didn't react at all. Richie guessed the joke wasn't as

funny as he thought. "Anyway," he continued. "The bones should keep her busy for a while. Hopefully long enough for us to get some answers to our questions about that bank."

Shay nodded. "Got it. I'd better get going. I tell you when I find anything."

They both stood. "Great. Thanks."

Shay abruptly left, and Richie returned to staring at his spreadsheets.

Shay got into the black Maserati parked in the alley behind Big Caesar's. The model was called "Quattroporte," which meant "four-door." For those who didn't know cars, it looked like a luxurious foreign sedan. For those who did know cars, it was a thing of pure beauty. A few years back, nine to be precise, he had told himself that one day he would be able to walk into an auto showroom and buy a Maserati or any other car he might want, and price would be no object.

Three years ago, he reached that goal.

But now, hearing Richie talk about a skeleton found in Golden Gate Park, he couldn't help but think of those days, shortly after he left the Marines, after he decided not to re-up as a sniper...

They were tough times, and because of that, the more Richie had talked about the skeleton, the more Shay had to drive over to the park and see the situation for himself.

He hoped he was being paranoid, but at the same time, he couldn't stay away. Nor could he let himself think about what such a discovery might mean.

Once near the park, he left his car and walked through foliage toward a location he remembered all too well.

His jaw ached from the way he had kept his teeth clenched

on the cross-city drive, and now, as he neared, his stomach tightened.

The bright yellow construction trucks came into view through the trees, and he noticed that much of the foliage and brush in the area had been cleared. His worst fear had just come true.

He drew in his breath and did his best to stay hidden behind pines as he inched closer.

An open trench was surrounded by heavy equipment, trucks, and stacks of new sewer pipes and manholes, all wrapped up inside crime scene tape.

Right now the trucks stood idle. A guard watched over the area, and several men and women in white coveralls crawled in and around the trench. Some had small shovels and plastic containers and seemed to be collecting samples of the soil. Another group was near mounds of dirt that had been taken from the trench.

Shay suspected they were crime scene technicians.

As he watched, Rebecca and her partner, Bill Sutter, approached the group. All of a sudden, the people in the trench became animated, and waved for the others to join them.

Shay's heart sank. He suspected what they had found.

5

After checking in at Homicide the next morning, Rebecca rode the elevator to the basement where the Medical Examiner's office was located.

Evelyn Ramirez got up from her desk as Rebecca entered. She looked as if she were dressed for an upscale business meeting, wearing an expensive gray suit, a light pink silk blouse, and rose pink high heels. But then she put on her white lab coat.

When they first met, Rebecca wondered why Evelyn dressed so nicely to work in this environment. She had since decided it was Evelyn's way to keep from becoming overwhelmed by the morbidity of cutting open people who had died under questionable circumstances. There was also the fact that she was an attractive, middle-aged divorcee. The way she presented herself meant she always had an entourage of admirers wherever she went, from "her" team of paramedics who would crawl through broken glass for her, to potential beaus.

"Have you had a chance to take a look at our 'boney Maronie'?" Rebecca asked.

"I have," Evelyn said as she opened the door to the morgue.

"He's quite fascinating—he is male, by the way. I've made an impression of his teeth. But I'm afraid I'm going to have to call in more people."

On the table lay the victim's bones—all placed where they should be, but unattached to each other. Rebecca drew in her breath. She had become used to dead bodies and autopsies—or as accustomed as any person could be to looking at the victims of abnormal and often violent death. But seeing a skeleton outside a laboratory was a whole new experience.

"More people?" Rebecca asked. "Why?"

"We have a problem." Evelyn put on gloves and picked up one of the victim's backbones, which Rebecca found strangely jarring. "The way this bone has fragmented indicates a bullet entered from behind." Evelyn ran her finger along the area she spoke of. "In other words, this victim very likely was shot in the back. From the angle of the trajectory, the bullet most likely struck his heart. So, I suspect we're looking at a murder. Based on that suspicion, we need to call in a few specialists to determine what happened to this man."

"You're talking about a team? Are you kidding me?" The cost, Rebecca knew, could be quite high.

"A team—I like the sound of that." Evelyn smiled. "We'll need the CSI, of course, but I'll also need a forensic anthropologist to help with body identification and reconstruction, a forensic odontologist to work with dental evidence, and a forensic entomologist to use insects to help determine the approximate time or, in this case, the year of death. We'll also need to collect all the DNA evidence possible around the crime scene." Evelyn again put the back bone onto the table.

Rebecca drew in her breath. "And that should help us identify who this is?"

"That's right. From the bones, teeth and DNA." Evelyn kept moving the bone a centimeter this way or that, trying to get it exactly where it needed to be.

"Any ideas now about the person's age, or how long he had been in the ground?" Rebecca asked.

"Definitely. But since I'm not an expert, it would be guesswork, and I'd hate to lead you astray."

Rebecca expected that answer. Evelyn hated to "guess" unless she was 99.9% certain she'd be proven right.

"My immediate interest," Evelyn said, removing the gloves, "comes from noting the bullet's entry wound, but not seeing a similar exit wound. Now, it's possible the bullet missed the rib cage and immediately exited through soft flesh, and if it did, we'll never know. But the more likely scenario is that the bullet remained inside the victim. Then, as the flesh and internal organs liquefied, the bullet would have slid out of the skeleton and onto the ground. I suspect it's still there. It easily could have ended up more deeply buried as the skeleton was lifted out of the ground, or as the construction equipment dug the trench, or even as the CSI walked over the soft dirt and caused it to shift."

"So you're saying we need to get back out there and dig around in the dirt that was under the skeleton?"

"As soon as possible, yes. The CSI already took some soil samples, but given the age and complete decomposition of this skeleton, I want them to take soil samples from up to three feet all around where the bones were found. My entomologist friend will use it to conduct some studies of the insects that are, or were, in and on the body." Evelyn gave a blissful sigh. "I envy him his knowledge. I've always wanted to do that!"

Rebecca didn't say anything, but she never ceased to be amazed by the strange things that excited Evelyn. Perhaps that was why, as much as she liked Evelyn, the two had never become really close friends.

Evelyn grabbed some papers she had stapled together and handed them to Rebecca. "You should read this. It's a fascinating article on how insect evidence will help us determine the post-mortem interval we're looking at."

Rebecca looked at the papers. "Great." She hoped she didn't sound sarcastic. "But, tell me, since years have passed, won't all the insects have gone on their merry insect way by now?"

"Ah, that's the beauty of forensic entomology." Evelyn smiled. "Their dead bodies leave evidence behind, just as the corpse's will have done. That's why we need the soil samples—to see exactly what died in it, and when."

"That's so weird, Evelyn."

"It's beautiful!" Evelyn exclaimed. "But I'm sure you can see that since the flesh decomposed and we're now at the skeletal stage, the forensics is complex to the point we need experts to help in our determinations. And, if this is a murder case, a qualified entomologist can offer court testimony."

"Good point," Rebecca said, then hesitated a moment. "Once you're done with all that, if we still can't identify the victim, is it possible to use a forensic artist to do a facial recognition drawing?"

Evelyn clasped her hands together. "Wouldn't that be fun? Could this case get any more fascinating?"

Rebecca certainly hoped not. For one thing, she was going to have to give all this information to Lt. Eastwood. The only thing he would see was that the case was growing more expensive by the hour.

That afternoon, Richie drove to Superior Savings Bank, and asked to speak to the assistant branch manager, Grant Yamada. Yamada immediately called him into in his office.

"I know who you are," Yamada said, standing behind his desk to receive Richie. He was a tall, broad Japanese-American, probably in his late fifties or early sixties. He didn't offer his hand. "Brian told me you visited him yesterday, and I remember how Isabella used to talk all the time about you. She was a wonderful woman, and I'm so sorry about what happened to her. I can understand that you're having trouble letting it go, and you want to continue to look into her death, to find answers, the 'why' of the accident. I'm sorry to say, Mr. Amalfi, but I've found that in life, at times, there simply are no answers. It was an accident after all."

Richie walked to the edge of the desk and eyed Yamada. Obviously, the man had expected him to show up, and had prepared the long speech. Unfortunately, it came across as more contrived than heartfelt. "You certainly have a lot to say about me and my life. But if there are any answers to be found, I'm going to do so. I'd like to know what you can tell me about the real estate holding company that had been owned by a woman named Audrey Poole. She was also a friend of mine, and she is also now dead."

"Ah, Audrey Poole," Yamada murmured. "Have a seat, please." He gestured toward the leather chair facing his desk. Richie took it.

"I remember Ms. Poole," Yamada said, settling back in his desk chair and folding his hands. "We serviced her holding company loans, but they were nothing special. San Francisco real estate is a major part of our business. We service an incredible number of such loans in this bank. It's what we do. I'm sorry to hear that Ms. Poole was also a friend of yours." Yamada cocked his head slightly as he looked at Richie. "Having known two women who have suffered untimely deaths, I can't help but suggest that perhaps the link is you, Mr. Amalfi, and not us. Coincidence runs both ways."

"I'll let that go," Richie said with a fierce glare. "I'll assume you're nervous, and you don't quite know what to say to me. So here's an easy question. Which of your employees was in charge of Audrey Poole's accounts?"

"Isabella, of course," Yamada's brows arched slightly even as his lips hinted at a smile. "She set them up, and after that, they needed little intervention from anyone. Perhaps... I hate to suggest it, but perhaps this is a rock you simply don't want to look under. Let your fiancée and her friend rest in peace."

Richie jumped to his feet. "What the hell are you implying?"

"You heard me, Mr. Amalfi." Yamada's voice was soft yet firm. He picked up a fountain pen and uncapped it. "Now, I'm a busy man, and if you have nothing specific to say to me I believe this conversation has ended."

Richie glared at Yamada and then stormed from the office. He didn't dare look back at the man who could make such disgusting insinuations; he feared what he might do to him.

∽

As Rebecca headed home, she found herself hoping to see Richie that evening. She hadn't seen or talked to him since he left her apartment two nights earlier ... and she missed him. She even missed those moments when his antics drove her mad.

She sighed heavily as she drove up Taylor Street, then tore her thoughts from Richie back to the case. She hated to admit it, but she found the skeleton very sad. She couldn't help but think that someone had lived with the hope that the missing man would return, and now, he never would. Or perhaps there was a worse scenario. That the man went missing, and no one cared.

Then, as ever, her thoughts drifted back to Richie. He always knew how to help her shed the blues—even if they were caused by a nameless, faceless collection of bones. She hoped that whatever had caused his strange behavior two nights earlier was now over, and he would be back to his old self.

She even hoped he might be in her apartment waiting for her.

But his car wasn't in the alley. Maybe he had parked somewhere legally, she told herself, even as she knew it wasn't likely. Her apartment was empty except for Spike. She greeted and hugged him, but he wasn't quite enough to chase away her unhappiness.

Her phone buzzed. She pulled it from her pocket, hoping it was Richie.

The phone's screen stopped her. Her day had just gone from bad to worse, and she debated about answering. The caller ID showed "Mom."

Lorene Mayfield and Rebecca had a poor relationship. They were cordial with each other, but little more. Rebecca had adored her father, Benjamin. He had owned a farm in Idaho and worked hard at it. He and Lorene separated when Rebecca was a teenager, and Lorene moved to Boise, taking Rebecca's younger sister, Courtney, with her. Rebecca chose to stay on the farm with her father. When his heart gave out at too young of an age, Rebecca's mother immediately sold the property.

Rebecca was age twenty-three at the time. Now, looking back, she could understand that running a farm without Ben would have been quite difficult for her. But she had resented that Lorene hadn't even consulted her before deciding to sell. One day, she had a home, a father, and a boyfriend with an "understanding about their future." The next, everything was gone.

Her sister, Courtney, had moved to Los Angeles right out of high school. She had always dreamed of becoming an actress, and she wasn't about to let anything get in the way of that. So, while Courtney couldn't care less what Lorene did, Rebecca cared. A lot.

The farm had been sold to Benjamin's brother, who was also a farmer. Her uncle said she could stay on with his family until she found a place to settle. He realized she might not be happy in the small city house Lorene had bought for herself.

Rebecca's steady boyfriend had lived on the farm adjacent to theirs. He was literally "the boy next door" that she had had a crush on while growing up and was thrilled when he finally started to notice her as something more than just some bothersome girl who liked to hang around him while he worked.

Once they started dating, everyone assumed they would marry and their farms would be joined. Even Rebecca had assumed it. But when her father's farm was sold, her beau seemed to lose all interest in their future.

Rebecca left the state and headed to San Francisco. She had surprised everybody, including herself, by getting accepted by the Police Academy. She joined the police department after graduation and found she actually loved the work. She never thought about returning to Idaho to live. Her home there was gone, and she had nothing left to go back to.

As the years went by, she grew further and further apart from Lorene. They'd talk on the phone around birthdays and holidays, and two or three other times during the year, but Rebecca rarely went to visit.

Guilt that she hadn't spoken with Lorene for some time filled her, and she answered the phone. "Mom, how are you?"

"I'm fine," Lorene said. "I'm calling to find out how *you're* doing."

"Me? Same old, same old," Rebecca said, wondering what brought that on.

"That's not the way I hear it," Lorene said. "Your sister called. Courtney said you're seeing a young man, and it's pretty serious."

Rebecca swallowed, remembering Courtney's strange visit to San Francisco a while back. "Oh, well—"

"Why didn't you tell me? Are there wedding bells in the future?"

"You know how Courtney exaggerates."

Silence. Then Lorene said, "I was afraid you'd say that. Did something happen between you and the fellow? Courtney worked hard to convince me you were actually serious about him. I told her you would have called to let me know if that was the case, but she insisted. She also said he was 'interesting,' but wouldn't tell me what that means. She said she'd let you explain. I guess that's not going to happen either."

Rebecca's teeth ached as she listened to Lorene's criticism. "You're right. It's not going to happen. There's nothing to explain. I am dating someone. But it's not a marriage situation. We're friends."

"You aren't saying he's already married, are you?" Lorene voice wavered between accusatory and resigned.

"No, I'm not saying that."

"Friends? All I can say is, if you like him, marry him. At your age, it's downright silly to hold out for someone you're madly in love with. Someone who'll turn your head and cause you to act in ways you never dreamed you would. Such love doesn't come along very often in real life, I'm sorry to say. Take your father and me. We were happy enough for quite a few years. Maybe my heart never beat faster when he was around, but he was a good man."

Rebecca knew exactly how little Lorene had cared about Benjamin and vowed she'd never marry rather than to be in a loveless marriage. Now, she feared blood would drip from her mouth the way she was biting her tongue. She chose to say nothing more about her love life, or how she felt about Richie.

If only you knew, Mom, she thought. Her feelings for him *were* the problem.

She pretended a call about a dead body had just come in and she ended the conversation.

Ready to spit nails, she plopped down on the sofa. Spike jumped up beside her, his big, bulging brown eyes questioning.

A part of her would have loved to have been able to tell her mother about Richie and how she felt about him. Instead, she had been reduced to, "It's not a marriage situation."

The thought struck that Richie must face similar questioning from his relatives nearly constantly since they were all over the city. She couldn't help but wonder if that was what had bothered him so much during their last get-together. Their relationship.

A short while back, she had told him she was miserable when not with him, and he said he felt the same. To her, that meant they should stay together because they enjoyed it, but that their "life choices," her being a cop and him being a "fixer" or whatever the less-loaded term was for his high-finance shenanigans, remained a problem.

In other words, there was no future, no "happily forever after" for them together.

It was a stupid idea, and she knew it the moment the words were out of her mouth.

And as far as actually living that way, it was hell.

She liked him, really, really liked him—maybe even more than she dared admit to herself. And she did want to think about a future with him. In other words, the time had come to "put up or shut up," "fish or cut bait," or whatever.

She decided to go to Big Caesar's that evening. There, she would face Richie and tell him how much she missed him, and ask if something was going on that they needed to talk about.

She started rummaging through her closet for something attractive to wear, but then stopped. Showing up at his nightclub in a bad mood and demanding to talk was not the way to handle Richie. He was probably still at home, so she picked up the phone and called before she got any other bright ideas.

He answered.

"Hi. How are you?" she asked, doing her best to sound upbeat and cheerful.

"Okay. Is everything all right?" He sounded surprised to hear from her.

"Fine. I'm just wondering what you're up to. Are you going to the club tonight? Are you very busy?" That couldn't be a clearer opening for an invitation.

"I am," he said. "I've got some personnel issues that need handling. I expect they won't leave me with time to deal with anything else tonight."

Deal with? "Oh, well, I guess I should let you go, then," she murmured. She could all but *feel* him withdrawing from her on the phone.

"Yeah. Well, good to talk to you. I'll give you a call soon, okay?"

"Sure."

With that, they said goodbye.

She stared at the phone. That wasn't Richie. Richie always had time to talk, and he definitely always had time for her. She wished she had done something to cause this reaction because then she would at least have something to try to fix. But now...

She couldn't stand it. Between Lt. Eastwood criticizing her at work, and now Richie acting weird, she was at her wit's end. She grabbed a bottle of chardonnay and headed up the back stairs to visit her neighbor, Kiki.

6

As Richie finished getting ready for work, he wondered about Rebecca's phone call. She sounded unhappy. He hated that he'd pretty much pushed her away. In time, he told himself, he'd make everything right again. But at the moment, he had too much going on that he wasn't ready to tell her about.

Before leaving the house, he picked up a case of Uncle Silvio's homemade wine from his basement, his usual "private reserve," and put it on the passenger seat of his Porsche. He then drove to a mansion in Presidio Heights, an area with homes of the rich and famous, including politicians, big business CEOs, the country's top attorneys, and one of the richest, most powerful men in the city's Italian community.

Giorgio Boiardi, called Don Giorgio, had headed a "West Coast operation" until he was sent to prison in 1989. He remained there until 2005 when he was released due to age and infirmity.

Once out of prison, Don Giorgio had rallied. In fact, Richie met Rebecca while trying to help some of Don Giorgio's old friends attend his ninetieth birthday party.

Now, Richie walked to the front door of the man who was

once *il capo di tutti capi*—the head honcho of all the heads of … well, Richie would prefer to not even think about what Giorgio Boiardi once headed. Anyway, all that was gone now. The one thing age and imprisonment did for Don Giorgio was to convince him to walk the straight and narrow. He might totter a bit from time to time, but the last thing he wanted was to be locked up again. He often said that those people who declared prisons to be like country clubs should spend a night in one.

Holding the wine, Richie rang the bell. An old man answered.

"*Signore* Amalfi, *benvenuto!*"

"*Grazie,* Alfonso. Is Signore Boiardi available?"

"*Sì, sì.* Come inside. *Prego!*"

"I have a little something for him," Richie said, indicating the wine he carried.

"Ah, *molto gentile!*" He took the wine and headed down the hall.

The living room was large for an older San Francisco home and was decorated in an old-fashioned European style with dark wood and ornate gold and green fabrics on heavy draperies and furniture.

Richie sat on a gold brocade sofa, one leg jiggling nervously.

Alfonso brought him a small cup of espresso. Richie added about three teaspoons of sugar and then drank it down quickly.

After a short wait, Boiardi entered the room. Anyone looking at him would see a small, frail man with whispery white hair, and have no idea of the power he once wielded throughout the San Francisco Bay Area and as far-reaching as Sacramento. "Eh, Richie! *Come va?*"

"*Tutto bene.*" Richie assured him all was well as he walked over to him. They hugged and kissed on both cheeks as Boiardi thanked him for the wine.

"It's been a long time, Richie," Boiardi said. "I thought you'd forgotten about me."

"Never, Don Giorgio," Richie said.

"*Bene.*" Don Giorgio sat in a tall, green velvet armchair, and Richie returned to the sofa. Boiardi continued, "I heard you've been spending most of your time with a pretty homicide detective. That's good, Richie, I'm happy to hear it."

"Thank you, Don Giorgio," Richie said, remembering how Don Giorgio had been there for him after Isabella's passing. "Actually, Rebecca is the reason I'm here."

"Oh?"

"Not long ago, she was called out to investigate a phony homicide, and someone tried to kill her. I suspect it was an inside job, and I'm worried they'll try again."

At the words "tried to kill her," Boiardi's dark brown eyes sparkled. "Ah, *molto interessante*. An inside job? But why? She's a cop. To kill her, that would cause big trouble."

"She was looking into a case that involved a lot of foreign money coming into the city—phony real estate deals. Next thing we know, she ended up a target. She was lucky to survive."

"She thinks her boss is in on it?" Boiardi asked.

"Not really. He's a new guy transferred up here from LA. He thinks he's going to become Chief of Police if he does the right thing, but frankly, he doesn't know shit from Shinola about the city or its politics."

Boiardi chuckled at Richie's old-fashioned expression, one Richie had heard him use many times over the years. "So, you're thinking, maybe she knows too much about these deals and someone higher up is afraid of the consequences."

"Exactly." Richie's jaw tightened. "Someone in the police department or City Hall. While I doubt her boss is a part of it, I think he's being pressured, and he's folding like an old cot. I want to find out who's after her and stop whoever it is."

"*Capito.* I'll see what I can learn." Boiardi nodded. "A couple guys I know, they still have ties with the mayor's office, and not much happens in this city that the mayor doesn't know about. Although, to be honest, most of the guys I used to work with, they're dead or they're so old and senile they just sit around and drool. Worthless, that's what they've become. It's not like the good ol' days, Richie. Still, for you, I'll see what I can do."

"*Grazie mille,* Don Giorgio."

He pointed a bony finger at Richie. "In the meantime, if these guys are as high up as you think, keep away from them. *Capish'?*"

"Okay, I understand."

"*Ascoltami!*"

"I hear you. I'll be careful."

The don stood, and so did Richie. They gave each other a quick hug, and Richie left for Big Caesar's. He was pleased with the visit, although he'd be damned if he was going to sit around doing nothing while Rebecca was in danger.

∼

Rebecca's upstairs neighbor, Kiki Nuñez, had been busy the past few weeks setting up a new day spa. She had to close her prior spa, Kiki's House of Beauty, after a body was found dead in a mud bath. Kiki suspected that no matter how much she swore the bath had been cleaned, customers willing to get into it would be few and far between. San Francisco might have its oddities, but so far they hadn't extended to ghoulish sloshes in the mud.

"Becca, you're a life saver!" Kiki said as she opened the backdoor to find Rebecca standing there with a bottle of chilled chardonnay in hand. "Just what I need! This spa business is killing me."

"Glad to be of service," Rebecca said as Kiki took the wine

bottle and poured them each a full glass, then put out some brie and crackers. Kiki was in her late forties, vivacious and outspoken. She had just gotten home from another tiring day moving furniture, unpacking supplies, and staging everything in a way that should be both handy and logical in the new spa.

They sat down in the living room. Kiki kicked off her shoes.

"What's wrong, Becca," Kiki said after taking a sip and letting the cool wine trickle down her throat. "You look like you lost your last friend."

"It's almost that bad," Rebecca said. "I just talked to my mother."

"Oh, I'm sorry!" Kiki said. In the past, Rebecca had told her the way Lorene found Rebecca to be a failure, and a disappointment compared to her "television-star" sister. For a few years Courtney did have a good, high-paying, on-going role in a daytime soap. But then her character was killed off. Her last job was as a zombie on *Walking Dead*. It didn't last long. But Courtney had faith that things would turn around for her, and so did Lorene. Compared to that, being a mere homicide detective was low on the prestige totem pole. "At least Richie will cheer you up," Kiki added.

"Hah!" Rebecca told her about his last visit, and her troublesome phone call. "It's so ironic. Just as I was thinking I trusted my feelings and his, and that it was safe to move things to the next level, he starts acting as if I'm the last person he wants to see. I always suspected it would happen eventually. But that doesn't make it any easier." She took a big swig of wine.

"These men!" Kiki said with disgust. "I thought better of him—and his friend Gino the Nailer."

"Oh, that's right. Gino was helping you with the spa," Rebecca said. "How did that work out?"

"It didn't. I thought he was called 'the Nailer' because he's such a good carpenter. I'll admit he was nice enough for a while, but he wanted more than money in payment for his assistance! That was what his nickname *really* referred to, son of a bitch! I threw him out."

Rebecca couldn't help but laugh. She could imagine Kiki tossing delusional Gino out on his ear. "I'm sorry to hear it. Richie should have known better than to recommend someone like that."

"I can't fault Richie. He got me such a good deal when I left my old spa, he'll have to murder someone in front of my eyes before I'll ever say a bad thing about him. But Gino! Bah! And here I thought he was special."

"You did?"

"Yeah. He is awfully cute and has a good sense of humor. But so what? His attitude was for the birds, so I told him *adios*. Still, it's disappointing."

"I'm sure someone special is out there for you, Kiki."

"Maybe." Kiki realized both glasses were empty and refilled them. "For all I know, Gino is still married. In fact, he might have more than one wife out there. A bigamist. Leave it to me to pick 'em!"

"Maybe he'll get a divorce."

"Maybe he's not over her yet," Kiki said. "Like Rich—, I mean, you know these guys." Kiki reached for her wine and took a big swallow.

"Like Richie?" Rebecca pounced. "What do you mean? Richie was never married."

"No. I know." Kiki vigorously shook her head.

"Engaged," Rebecca said, closely studying Kiki.

"Yeah, I heard." Kiki studied her wineglass as she swirled the wine in it.

Rebecca frowned. "Did Gino tell you Richie's not over Isabella yet or something? Did you two talk about Richie being unable to forget her?"

Kiki put down the glass. "No, Becca! Nothing like that! Richie loves you, I'm sure. Don't think otherwise. It's just that..."

"*That?*"

"Gino told me he's looking into her death."

It took a second for Rebecca to comprehend what Kiki was saying. "What do you mean? It was a car accident. What's there to look into?"

Kiki shrugged helplessly. "Apparently, he heard something from an old girlfriend." Kiki's mouth wrinkled. "Yeah, another old girlfriend. I hadn't really thought about it before, but the guy really is like Casanova, isn't he? Anyway, he was talking to some old girlfriend, and she told him something that made him wonder if his old fiancée got too close to some high finance thing going on that involved a bunch of big shots in the city. Isn't that weird? How one old girlfriend would tell him something about another that would cause him to go all Inspector Clouseau? I mean, if he was over his fiancée, he'd let it go, wouldn't he? I'm only telling you this because I don't want you to be hurt any more than I think you already are."

"Thanks." Rebecca's tone conveyed anything but gratitude.

"I mean it. I admit I was the one pushing you toward him all the time, even as you thought you should stay away. Well, I'm changing my tune. If he's so hung-up that he's going off half-cocked because of something he heard, I don't think you want to get any more involved with him."

"I appreciate your concern, Kiki." Rebecca had to change the subject or she might not be able to hold in how upsetting Kiki's words were to her. She chugged down the glass of wine and forced a smile. "Now, tell me what your latest plans are for the new spa."

But Rebecca only half listened to her friend's plans. Her mind was racing. Try as she might to keep thoughts of Richie at bay, she couldn't help but think that he was stirring up things that could have consequences for both of them—and none of them pleasant.

7

Rebecca was running late the next morning as she drove to work. She was approaching an intersection, hoping the light wouldn't change before she crossed it. The car in front of her slowed down.

"Idiot! The light's still green!" she shouted, even though she knew the driver couldn't hear her. But then the driver made a turn onto Jones Street.

The light switched to yellow as she continued into the intersection. From the corner of her eye, she saw a huge Mack truck barreling toward her. His light was still red, but it didn't look like he had any intention of stopping.

She stomped hard on the gas, but braced for the collision.

∽

The Homicide Department of the Bureau of Inspections was located on the fourth floor of the Hall of Justice. It consisted of one large room where the inspectors had their desks. Along the perimeter were Lieutenant Eastwood's office, interrogation rooms, and a small reception area where the staff's administrative assistant sat.

"What's wrong with drivers these days?" Rebecca fumed at Bo Benson as she flung herself into her desk chair. Bo sat near her and was her closest friend on the staff. A couple of years younger than Rebecca, he was single, handsome, and African-American, with a quiet, wicked sense of humor when he let it show.

"It's a war zone out there, that's what's wrong. Why?" Bo asked. "You get too many one-fingered salutes or something?"

"Let them try it," she said with a huff is she smoothed her hair and sat. "A truck, a big one, nearly ran into me. Luckily, the car in front of me had turned the corner, so I was able to hit the gas and get out of its way. If that car hadn't turned, I wouldn't have had any room to maneuver!"

Bo looked askance at the implication of her description. "You'd have been broadsided. That's not good."

"No. You'd be peeling me and my car off his grill."

At this point, Inspector Paavo Smith was also listening. Paavo was married to Richie's cousin, Angie. Rebecca once had a "thing" for Paavo, but he had eyes only for Angie. "Were you able to see his license plate or if there was a company name on the truck?" Paavo asked.

"I didn't even notice him until I was in the intersection, and then, all of a sudden, he was on top of me. If he missed me by more than two inches, I'd be surprised."

"Strange," Bo said. "I wonder if he'd been parked and then pulled onto the street just as you started to drive by. Maybe I'll see if your bad driver showed up on a traffic cam. Such a jerk might merit a message of concern about his driving."

"Maybe," Rebecca said thoughtfully. "At least no harm was done, but that is not the way to start one's day. Is Sutter here yet?" Paavo and Bo shook their heads. "Okay, tell him I'm downstairs. I've got to see if I can push the ME to move a little faster on our skeleton. While I'm there, I might stop in at the morgue and pretend that maniac truck driver is on one of the slabs."

Bo chuckled. "Sounds like the milk of human kindness just curdled."

～

Shay wasn't surprised that Richie was phoning him before noon. Richie wanted the investigation into Superior Savings Bank over with as soon as possible, saying "other things" had come up that he'd like Shay to handle, but not until the bank investigation was completed.

It wasn't as if Shay had been purposely procrastinating, but he wanted all the data and facts nailed down before he told Richie anything more about what had happened. This situation was too important for him to rush, despite Richie's anxiety about what might be discovered.

Shay also wondered how long it would be before Rebecca phoned to ask what was going on with Richie. Shay couldn't help but hope Richie would get a nice big situation to "fix" for one of his wealthy clients. Those were the cases Shay liked to research. Not these with so much emotion attached to them.

Years ago, Shay had learned to put aside his emotions. He had learned he had few needs in life. Housing, food, and something to occupy his mind. And he also learned that with enough money he could set up a barrier between himself and others—that he would never again have to subject himself to the wayward or inane emotions of other people, or even himself. He set out, nine years earlier, to amass enough money to live on as he wanted. And he had met that goal.

He found life a lot easier this way. No attachments, no feelings. Just simple, smooth sailing.

He tossed aside the research he had been doing. The bank's handling of the real estate holding company, per se, wasn't the problem. It was legal. The problem was that the company had been used fraudulently.

Since all the bank's records of the now deceased Audrey Poole's company had been wiped off its database, Shay was certain someone at Superior Savings was involved in the illegal enterprise. He needed to discover who.

But, he reminded himself, despite that, he saw nothing to implicate anyone at the bank in Isabella Russo's death.

He got up from his desk. Playing with the bank's database held zero interest for him today. He'd go back to it eventually, as he'd promised ...

Not that he'd made the promise because he liked Richie. Or Vito. Or that they were the only people he ever talked to or met outside his home. They provided stimulation and interest for him, that's all. And he definitely didn't need Richie's money.

He didn't need anything from anyone.

Life, he told himself, was good.

He walked to the window and gazed at a quiet street near Julius Kahn Park along the southern edge of the Presidio, a former army base turned recreation area. It was in one of the city's wealthiest neighborhoods, and his home had once been a mansion. He had converted its top floor into a large, beautiful two-bedroom apartment with a library, den, formal dining room, and maid's quarters. He never used the dining room, but he enjoyed having it, nonetheless.

The bottom floor of the home had been converted into two small but extremely nice apartments, one rented by a single man who worked in the city's financial industry, the other by a single woman who worked for Google. Both stayed out of his way, allowing him to go about his days and nights with no contact whatsoever with either of them. That was the only type of tenant he would allow. Others who hadn't met that standard soon found themselves moving out. Despite the city's rent control and strong support of tenant's rights, he hadn't come across anyone willing to argue with him when he told them they had three days to leave the premises.

Because his apartment was large, and Shay was more than a little fussy, he employed a full-time housekeeper. Mrs. Brannigan was a widow, in her sixties, who cooked the way he liked it, kept his clothes immaculate, and the house spotless. She also had a sense of humor, and when he fussed too much, she'd tell him he was lucky he wasn't married because any wife would poison his food before she put up with such nonsense.

That always took him aback. He didn't see himself as being nonsensical at all. What most intrigued him was that where most people were afraid of him, Mrs. Brannigan wasn't in the least bit intimidated. That, he realized, was a good reason to keep her around.

He stepped out to a small balcony off the living room. As usual, the wind was up and a chill filled the air. He hoped it would clear his head because the only thing he found himself truly able to think about was the skeleton that Rebecca was trying to identify.

8

That evening, just as Richie had done the night before, he made a detour before going to Big Caesars—actually more than a detour, a cross-city jaunt. He now found himself ringing the doorbell of a mid-century modern home in the exclusive Sea Cliff district. He had contacted his cousin Angie to be sure she and her husband, Homicide Inspector Paavo Smith, would be home before he drove all the way out to the western edge of the city. It wasn't really all that far, but to Richie, who spent most of his time in the chaotic hubbub surrounding Fisherman's Wharf, North Beach, and the crowded Nob Hill-Tenderloin morass where Rebecca lived, this area was so quiet it could be a cemetery, the houses nothing but mausoleums. He wondered how Angie stood it. She was his favorite cousin, warm, funny, and always active, as well as a bit of a busy-body. But a warm-hearted busy-body, he had to admit. He also knew she probably spent a lot of time alone. As he had learned dating Rebecca, the life of a homicide detective wasn't his or her own. It was a nightmare of phone calls that seemed to come in at the least opportune times.

He hated to think of how many great evenings with Rebecca

had been ruined because some jerk managed to get himself killed. Homicide's dispatcher was the most reliable form of *coitus interruptus* he'd ever encountered.

If he was smart, he'd dump Rebecca and her crummy job. But he wasn't smart. Not where Rebecca was concerned. As much as he hadn't wanted it to happen, she'd come to mean too much for him to even think about walking away. Somehow, she'd become a big part of his life.

For that reason, he'd come up with a plan. A man with a plan—that was him, Richard Joseph Francis Amalfi. And he was working to put that plan into action.

That was why he was here.

Angie opened the front door. She looked pretty as ever, with her highlighted short brown hair, big brown eyes, and petite figure clad today in a green jumpsuit with a wide belt. "Richie, welcome!" she cried as she wrapped her arms around him and kissed his cheek. He greeted her the same way.

"I'm so glad you've come over. You haven't seen the house, yet. Isn't it pretty?"

He walked into a nice size living room with a fireplace on one wall and sliding glass doors that gave a view of the Pacific. "Very nice," he said, then caught Paavo's eye. "Paavo, good to see you."

Paavo sat on a sofa, his laptop computer and a bottle of beer on the coffee table, papers all around him, and jazz playing in the background. "You, too. Like a beer?"

"After the tour," Angie said as she looped her arm in Richie's and pulled him through the house. He had heard that Angie found the house for a very good price because it was supposedly haunted. Since he had no belief whatsoever in ghosts, if he'd heard that a place as nice as this one, in one of the city's best neighborhoods, was for sale cheap, he'd have snapped it up in a heartbeat. As he looked around, he gained a whole new respect for his cousin's financial smarts.

As much as he appreciated the tour, as much as he enjoyed looking out at the expansive view of the Pacific, he'd come here for a reason, and was glad to get back to the living room. Paavo handed him a beer as Richie took a seat.

"I'm trying to get our finances under some kind of order," Paavo said by way of explanation of all the paperwork. "Buying a house is bad enough, but then remodeling and furnishing it is even worse."

Richie nodded and smiled, but didn't say a word. Angie's father was loaded, and he made sure all five of his daughters had their own trusts. *Not to worry, Paavo.*

Angie soon appeared with a tray of taquitos and quesadillas, along with guacamole, salsa, and tortilla chips. She sat down on the sofa beside Paavo. Richie bit into a homemade quesadilla, one of Angie's always delicious concoctions. Paavo was one lucky guy to have married such a great cook.

After some inconsequential chit-chat, it became clear that both Paavo and Angie were wondering what brought him to their home.

He got to it. "I'm here to talk to you about Rebecca," he said to Paavo.

Paavo nodded. "I suspected as much. You two see a lot of each other, I hear."

"Yes. And I care about her a lot."

Angie beamed at him. "I knew it," she cried, clasping her hands. "Have you proposed yet?"

"No. That's not it at all." Richie's voice was stern.

Angie's face fell. "Sorry."

Richie turned to Paavo. "I'd appreciate it if you don't tell Rebecca I've talked to you about this, but she thinks Eastwood wants her out of Homicide."

Paavo looked taken aback. "They have their differences, but I didn't think it had gone that far."

"She's wondering if her career is over," Richie said. "And if so, I don't know if she should be encouraged to stick it out, or if she should leave? Or, since I know Eastwood doesn't care for me, is her seeing me why her boss's nose is out of joint?"

"It's not the latter," Paavo's brow furrowed. "But why does she think her career is over? She's a good cop and has a terrific closure rate on her investigations. That's what tends to be important."

"It has to do with the mayor's chief-of-staff's suicide. Apparently, the mayor blames Rebecca. And she doesn't believe it was suicide, but Eastwood closed the investigation."

Paavo shook his head. "I know Eastwood's ambitious, but he's got a reputation as a good investigator. I can't imagine he'd go along with the mayor if he didn't believe he was right."

"You can't, or you don't want to 'imagine' it?" Richie asked, his tone hard.

"Richie, relax," Angie said, reaching over to put her hand on his arm. "Paavo wants to help you both."

"You make a good point," Paavo said. "None of us knows Eastwood that well. All I can say is, I'll try to find out what's going on there."

Richie visibly relaxed. "Good. I appreciate it."

"Frankly," Paavo continued, "I thought you were worried about her nearly being killed. It was a weird situation."

Richie stared at him. "What are you talking about?"

"This morning. On the way to work. Didn't she tell you? She was furious, but if that truck had broadsided her..."

"*What truck?*"

Paavo quickly told him what little he knew.

"Damn! That's proof she's in danger," Richie said. "We've gone from the mayor wanting her fired, to somebody putting warnings on her car and front door, to her being nearly killed. What the hell is going on?"

"That's terrible," Angie cried. "Paavo can't you do something?"

"This is the first I've heard about any of it," Paavo said. "What worries me are the threats—and her not telling anyone."

"I wouldn't know either if I hadn't found one myself on her front door. Damn it, Paavo, she blew it off, said I was making a big deal out of nothing."

"She's in denial," Paavo said.

"She'd kill me if she knew I told you."

"I'll be keeping an eye on her."

"Yeah, well," Richie rubbed his temples, "good because that partner of hers is worthless. I wish he would just retire."

"He's an okay guy," Paavo said. "And he really does try to watch out for her. All of us do our best to watch out for each other."

"I'd feel better if I didn't think he'd have to move his walker out of the way before he could draw his gun," Richie said with a sneer.

"Ouch," Angie said.

"He's not that bad," Paavo insisted. "Still, if there is a problem, I don't think it's with Eastwood but with someone a lot higher up. You're the one with the connections in City Hall, Richie."

"I'm covering that angle," Richie said. "But I can't watch Homicide and the SFPD brass. I need to be sure you've got her back."

Paavo nodded. "I do; you can be sure of it."

Angie leaned over and put her hand on Richie's shoulder. "Rebecca has you looking out for her, and she's got Paavo. She couldn't do better."

"Thanks, Angie," Richie said, then grimaced. "Now, if I could only convince Rebecca of that, maybe we'd all be happy."

∽

Shay drove through the fog-filled streets as memories flooded over him, memories of how it had all turned out so wrong, of how he had walked away and never looked back...

He couldn't believe he was doing this now. But here he was.

He knew better than to drive to a certain street, but he couldn't stop himself. Not after learning that what he'd feared all these years had come to pass.

The irony of it was, he couldn't decide if he did or didn't want to be there.

If he was smart, he'd make a U-turn and head for home as fast as his Maserati could travel. What kind of jerk was he?

Perhaps the kind who wanted to make sure a woman he had once loved was fine, and that her life was a happy one now.

He saw a parking space a couple of houses before hers on the opposite side of the street. He took it. Maybe if he just sat here a while, contemplating what "normal" looked like—as in the normal life she was living now—he could convince himself to never come back here again. It had all happened long ago. The damned corpse was a skeleton now. No one, not even Rebecca Mayfield could figure out who he was. Or why he had been placed in that lonely, unmarked grave.

The home was small as were all these in the Oceanview neighborhood. No car was parked in the driveway, and the drapes were drawn on its front rooms. That was the way homes looked during the day when the couple living there worked outside the home, and when the children, if any, were in school or daycare.

For some inexplicable reason, the knowledge comforted him and also made him realize he should leave. Earlier, as he drove here, he had considered ringing the doorbell and giving her a warning that her life might suddenly change. That long held dangers and secrets might be revealed.

But now, he couldn't do that to her. If she was lucky, nothing would come of the discovery. But luck had never been her strong suit. Perhaps, as always, the solution would be up to him.

He was about to start his car to head back home when he saw a Buick sedan turn onto the street heading towards him. He decided to wait; to let it pass. No sense drawing attention to himself. His Maserati drew enough attention from people who knew cars.

But the car he saw didn't continue along the street. Instead, it slowed and pulled into the driveway of her house. A man was at the wheel, she sat in the passenger seat, and a child—perhaps more than one—sat in the back.

The garage door automatically opened, and the car disappeared into its maw. Slowly, the door lowered, closing off the family from his view.

His breathing came hard and fast. He hadn't been able to see her all that well. Only in profile. But he knew that profile. He would never forget it.

Nice car, nice home, a family. What else did he expect?

He sat there a while longer and then drove back to his empty apartment.

9

"Vito, there's something going on with the Inspector," Richie said into his phone the next morning. For some reason, Vito Grazioso, Richie's friend and "muscle," always referred to Rebecca as "the Inspector" instead of by name. He even had Richie doing it when they spoke.

"What do you want me to do, boss?" Vito asked.

Good question. Richie had spent most of last evening while at Big Caesar's mulling over Paavo's story of a truck nearly crashing into Rebecca. Then, that morning, Paavo called with the news that the traffic cam showed a truck with no visible markings or license plate. The driver not only wore oversized sunglasses and a baseball cap, but kept his head bent in a way that caused the brim of the cap to cover most of his face.

Richie was outraged. And worried.

He wouldn't have thought real estate was a reason for killing, but the mayor's own chief-of-staff seemed to have been the recipient of an assisted suicide—and the assistance wasn't performed by his doctor, or at his request. The fact that Rebecca had once dated the staffer caused Richie to think she had amazingly poor taste in men—before she met him, of course.

"I need you to keep an eye on her and her apartment," Richie said. "Someone left warning messages on her front door and her car windshield, and then yesterday, someone tried to broadside her with a truck. Take some of that surveillance equipment you've got and string it up so we can watch her apartment in case our messenger pays a repeat visit. But most of all, you need to be ready to act if someone tries to hurt her. She can be pretty hard to surveil —especially if she notices you and throws a fit. But at least try. She's making someone very nervous, and I want to know who."

"Anything for you, boss," Vito said. "And the Inspector."

～

As Rebecca sat at her desk, she realized the only interesting case she had was a skeleton. Everything else involved writing reports and filling out paperwork.

She knew Dr. Ramirez was having a great time working with the team of specialists, but they had nothing to give Rebecca as yet. Evelyn refused to speculate on how many years the body had been buried out there. Was it five years or fifty? Rebecca could somewhat understand her recalcitrance. After all, she had called in forensic specialists. If her own guesses were way off from what the "experts" eventually determined, that could undermine her credibility in the future—and her self-esteem.

The delay gave Rebecca an excuse to turn her attention to the issue that had been on her mind ever since her conversation with Kiki.

She headed down to the Records Unit to access the report on the fatal accident that had killed Isabella Russo. The Records Unit directed her to the traffic section. There, she found out the exact date of the accident, four and a half years earlier. She handed the desk clerk a request for the file.

The file was surprisingly thin. She hesitated to take it up to her desk. If anyone saw her with it, they would ask questions—questions for which she had no good answers.

She found a corner of the records office, pushed a chair into it, and sat. With the file on her lap, she began to read.

The first thing she saw were photographs. They were difficult to look at. The once beautiful woman took the brunt of the accident to the head and face, despite the seatbelt and airbag—an airbag that hadn't opened for some unknown reason. Isabella had been pronounced dead at the scene.

Rebecca knew the area where the accident had taken place. It was a mixture of open roadway and tunnels leading to the Golden Gate Bridge. Isabella's car was inside the tunnel going at such a high speed that when it failed to negotiate a slight curve, it jumped the low cement barricade at the foot of the tunnel walls, and hit the wall head on. Skid marks indicated she had tried braking, but she did it much too late. It appeared her car may have been hit by others as well, but if so, those other cars fled the scene. The accident had happened just before six in the morning. Six o'clock, Rebecca thought, the break of a new day, and also the time when Richie's world suddenly turned bitter, cold, and silent.

She forced herself to read on.

Several people reported what looked like a stalled car or an accident from their cell phones as they passed by.

The month was January, so the sky was still dark that time of the morning. The fog was heavy, and the thick mist had drifted inside the tunnel. The authorities speculated that the fog may have caused Isabella not to see how the roadway curved and she continued to drive straight ahead. Or, more likely, she simply fell asleep at the wheel.

Strangely, a 911 call logged at 5:55 a.m. had reported two

vehicles recklessly speeding along the Marina Green, a street that led to the bridge approach. The caller said the police needed to slow those cars down before anyone got hurt, and then he hung up before giving any more information, including his name.

Apparently, no one had looked into the call, or it had led to a dead end.

Rebecca then turned to brief interviews with Isabella's family, including Richie. None of them had any idea where she might have been going, or why she would have been leaving the city at that time of the morning.

Next were contacts with Isabella's friends and then with her employer.

Oh, my God! As Rebecca read the employer's name, she suddenly understood Richie's renewed interest in Isabella's death—Superior Savings Bank. It had come up just a few weeks earlier as she investigated several murders involving, among others, Audrey Poole, one of Richie's old girlfriends. Poole had set up a scam real estate holding company, and her bank was Superior Savings.

And, Rebecca thought, loan officers dealt with real estate loans.

Were they all connected: Audrey Poole, Isabella Russo, and Richie?

No. Rebecca was letting her wary cop brain get ahead of her rational side. Richie had decided to look into Isabella's death because he *hadn't* known there was any connection between Isabella and Audrey's holding company.

He had to have been as stunned by the news as Rebecca. Why, she wondered, hadn't he told her about any of this?

Instead, he was looking into the situation alone—suspicious about what happened out there on the Golden Gate Bridge approach in those early morning hours.

Rebecca could understand why.

She turned back to the file and learned that Isabella had never even gotten a traffic ticket.

She gazed again at scenes from the accident and hoped Richie never saw them. She looked for some hint as to why the airbag hadn't deployed, but it was just put down as a malfunction. An ironically timed malfunction, Rebecca thought, but she understood from people who worked traffic accidents, that the bags weren't 100% reliable.

Isabella had no alcohol, drugs, or medicines in her system. It wasn't possible to test for falling asleep, and that was the investigators' best reason for the accident. It would explain why she hadn't turned the wheel, and that she might have woken up only at the last second and stomped on the brakes at that point.

There wasn't much else in the files. Rebecca looked for the name of the investigating officer. Jim Taylor was part of the SFPD's Special Operations Branch's Traffic Company. One of the branch's duties was to investigate traffic accidents. This was the sort of accident that stuck with a person. She borrowed the clerk's computer to do a quick check to see if Jim Taylor still worked Traffic.

He had retired four years earlier.

10

At six o'clock that evening, as Rebecca once again parked her car atop a red "no parking" zone near her apartment, she scanned the street for Richie's black Porsche. It wasn't anywhere to be seen. Disappointment struck. Four days had passed since she last saw him. Not that she was counting.

With each step she took toward her apartment, she hoped Richie had parked somewhere else, that he'd be on the other side of the door when she walked into the flat, but it wasn't her nearly six-foot, oh-so-handsome Italian who greeted her, but Spike. He bounded from the sofa where Richie so often sat and jumped into her arms, plying her chin with kisses. She hugged the little guy and kissed him back. Still, she couldn't help but wish it was Richie in her arms.

But only memories of Richie filled the room, and those memories weren't nearly enough.

She and Spike went out to the backyard, and she played fetch with him a while. Back indoors, she gave Spike his Alpo dinner, then made herself ramen and a tossed salad, paired with a piece of Popeye's Chicken from the night before. But she only nibbled at the food, offering bits and pieces to Spike.

She had finished eating, and was putting her dishes in the dishwasher, when there was a knock on her door.

She guessed one of her upstairs neighbors, Kiki Nuñez or Bradley Frick, had come down the backstairs to visit with her. The best thing about her tiny apartment was that it opened to a backyard with plants and benches. Since her upstairs neighbors rarely used the yard, it felt as if it were her own private garden. She and Spike loved it.

Her heart leapt when she opened the front door and found Richie standing there, but she couldn't throw herself into his arms. He wasn't alone. One of his best friends, a worrisome fellow who called himself Shay was at his side. For a reason never explained to Rebecca, Shay didn't like using his real name, Henry Ian Tate, III. In fact, despite his outrageously good looks, with lush blond hair and blue eyes tinged with a hint of lavender, his gaze was so cold he looked like he could chisel stone with a mere glance. Rebecca didn't know anything about his background, but she suspected words like "sniper," "CIA," and even "contractor," had to be a part of it. She also found it ironic that his initials were HIT, as in "hit man."

But then, her gaze hurried back to Richie, and the memory of the accident file and of the photos she had seen that afternoon struck. Despite everything, her heart went out to him for the loss he had suffered.

He looked at her strangely, as if reading that something was wrong, and she forced a small smile to her lips. "What a surprise this is," she said with a lilt. "Come in."

She held open the door as they entered. The two men were an interesting study in contrast, Richie with his dark good looks, exuding warmth and emotion, while Shay's fair demeanor was one of unflinching iciness. At the same time, both dressed impeccably and shared tall, slim good-looks. More than once, Rebecca had watched women cease all conversation to gawk when the two entered a bar, nightclub, or even an inexpensive café.

"Can I get you something?" she asked, uncomfortable with the formality that was keeping them apart. "A beer perhaps, or some wine?"

"Beer would be good." Richie's voice sounded all too businesslike. He took off his jacket and threw it over the back of the sofa.

"Ice water for me." Shay said. He removed one of the ever-present ascots he wore and placed it on a coat hook by the door. He left his jacket on.

Rebecca got the drinks while Spike greeted Richie exuberantly and even allowed Shay to pat his head. Rebecca found her little dog's lack of discernment disturbing at times.

"I told Shay about the skeleton that had been dug up in the sewer trench," Richie said, as Rebecca took a bottle of beer from the fridge. "He was fascinated by the new techniques that might allow you to ID a bunch of bones."

She studied Shay. Richie's words didn't ring true. Shay knew far more than most people about all kinds of investigative techniques whether legitimate or not. "I had no idea you were interested in such things," she said to Shay.

Rebecca brought a tray of drinks into the small living room, set it on the coffee table, and sat on the sofa with Richie.

Shay took the rocking chair near the heater. His cold eyes stared at her. "New police techniques always interest me. I take it no identification has been made yet."

"Not, yet," she said, reaching for the glass of pinot grigio she had poured for herself. "And, I'm sorry to disappoint, but the techniques being used aren't all that new. The only thing different is that Evelyn, that's Dr. Ramirez, the ME, called in a team of experts and together they're going over the skeleton. It seems to be a fun time for all of them. I guess these situations don't come up all that often."

"What are these techniques?" Shay asked.

Rebecca sipped some wine. Shay knew this stuff. What game was he playing? She debated not answering him, but that wouldn't get her anywhere. Maybe if she went along, she'd learn why he was asking. "I'm sure you've heard of the Combined DNA Index System, CODIS, used by federal, state and local law enforcement to exchange and compare DNA profiles."

"Sure," Shay muttered.

"Well, we now have the National Missing and Unidentified Persons System, called NamUs—an acronym too cute by half. Evelyn's forensic team will work out sex, race, and any distinctive body features to whatever degree possible. They'll then apply their findings against the various databases available."

"Yes, but you'll end up with a lot of similarities." Shay's tone was dismissive as he pushed a lock of hair off his forehead with a distracted rake of his fingers. "That technique leaves plenty of room for confusion and misnaming."

First, he asks me questions, and now he argues with my answers? "Not if we have a DNA match." Rebecca hoped she didn't sound as defensive as she felt.

"Well, of course. But if you don't?" he asked.

"Ease up, Shay," Richie said.

"It's all right, Richie." Rebecca folded her arms. "It's easy enough to answer. If we don't have a DNA match, we manually pare down the names using geographical location, when the person went missing, age, whatever. Once we have a workable number of possibilities, we use dental images from the skeleton, and go through dental records looking for a match. At that point, old-fashioned police work will identify the person. But you already know that, Shay. So why are you asking?"

His mouth tightened. "I'm just thinking that sounds like a lot of expense for a skeleton. Do you have any idea of the age yet? Could it be someone who died a century ago, for example? And if so, why does anyone care?"

"Okay," Richie interrupted again. "I think that's enough with the third degree."

Rebecca put her hand on Richie's arm. The more questions Shay asked, the more curious she became as to why he was so interested. "I don't mind the questions," she said. "Of course, I can't give out details about an open investigation, but in general terms, an entomologist looking at the insects and detritus around the cadaver should be able to give some idea as to dates involved—along with an examination of the bones themselves."

Shay's eyes narrowed. "You used the word investigation. Are you saying you suspect foul play?"

Rebecca pursed her lips. "I always suspect foul play."

"Well," Richie interrupted, clearly not liking the way this conversation was going. He faced Shay. "I suspect that answers your questions."

"It does," he replied.

"But Shay hasn't answered mine yet. Exactly, why are you curious about this case?" Rebecca asked.

Shay lifted those intense ice-blue eyes of his, but his focus was slightly off, as if he were looking past her. His gaze usually bothered her, but this evening she sensed pain in it, as if the coldness covered a deep trouble. No sooner had she thought that then his glare shifted to land directly and harshly her way. She guessed she'd been wrong. "It's not about *this* case," he growled. "It's research."

She nodded. "Of course. What else could it be?"

He stood. "Right. If you'll both excuse me, I've got some business to take care of."

Richie stood as well. "I should also get going. I've got some people I need to see." He looked even more troubled than Shay as he confessed, "I'm sorry about all this Rebecca. I ... I'll call you soon, okay?"

She wanted to put a hand on Richie's arm, to ask him to stay, but she held back. The man who'd spent so many hours in her apartment, in her arms, in her bed, and her life, had other things on his mind. Other things that didn't include her.

He gave Rebecca a quick, perfunctory kiss on the lips, then both men said their goodbyes and left.

Rebecca stood lonely and alone in her apartment replaying in her mind all that had just happened. She wasn't sure which of the two men troubled her more.

11

A little after eight o'clock the next morning, Dr. Evelyn Ramirez waltzed into Homicide and met Rebecca's gaze with a huge smile. Rebecca, along with the other detectives in the room at the moment—Sutter, Paavo, and Calderon—stared at her as if she were a creature from another planet. First, Evelyn rarely smiled, and secondly, she never, ever, left her basement lair to appear in Homicide or anywhere else in the Hall of Justice unless demanded to do so by court order.

"We did it!" Evelyn sang out as she marched forward waving a file folder over her head. "It came together much faster than I ever imagined. That's what happens when a great team is put together."

"You've got a name?" Rebecca asked hopefully.

"We do." She placed the folder squarely in the center of Rebecca's desk, atop the other papers Rebecca had been looking at. "He was missing, and now he's found. You can thank me with a glass of wine when you have time." With that, she breezed out again.

Rebecca opened the folder. Inside was the photo of the California driver's license showing a stocky man named Yussef

Najjar, with curly black hair, brown eyes, and a fleshy face. Looking at his birth date, if he were still alive, he would be forty-three years of age. He had died nine years earlier.

She quickly looked over the forensic reports from Evelyn's team of experts. There was no DNA match, but working with the NamUs records they were able to find a dental record match for the victim. There was no doubt as to his identity.

Rebecca then turned to the more interesting information—the missing person's investigation, which had been conducted nine years earlier by the San Mateo Police Department with some assistance from the Missing Person division of the SFPD's Special Victims Unit. San Mateo's involvement was a surprise. It was a small city about twenty miles south of San Francisco.

Dr. Ramirez had enclosed a copy of their investigation.

Nine years earlier, Najjar had been reported missing by his employer, the manager of a carpet warehouse in San Mateo. He said he had tried to reach Najjar for several days with no luck.

Najjar had given no information about his family to his employer, and it took the San Mateo investigators several days before they located someone who knew Najjar had relatives in San Francisco. The police went through the phone book, calling every Najjar listed. Najjar's mother answered one of their calls. They went to her, and she told them that Yussef Najjar had returned to Lebanon.

The officers reported that back to the employer and closed the case.

Rebecca had to wonder about this. It made no sense. If the mother thought he had left the country, why didn't she become concerned when she never heard from him again? Even if Najjar and his mother weren't close, as might have been the case, she should have had some contact with him over nine years' time, or have been worried that she had heard nothing.

It was, if anything, highly suspicious, and made Rebecca

suspect the mother knew from the beginning what had happened to Yussef Najjar.

She gave Sutter the material to read through. They decided that before they confronted the mother or anyone else in the family about Najjar's death, they wanted a little more information about him, the family, and even the ease of traveling into and out of Lebanon.

She began by searching for Najjar's status in the US and learned he was here as a permanent resident. Rebecca called Patti Flynn, a contact who worked with the US Department of State, to find out how to go about checking if Najjar had traveled to Lebanon. Also, she couldn't help but wonder if someone traveling to that country might not have been flagged by the Department of Homeland Security. From Flynn, she learned about the electronic "Advance Passenger Information System," one of many systems used by the State Department as well as Homeland Security to track certain international travelers.

Many such programs were not known to the public, and not available for public scrutiny. Rebecca gave Flynn all the information she had about Yussef Najjar, and Flynn said she would get back to Rebecca as soon as she found out anything.

∾

Ethan Nolan got off the number 41 Union Street bus and started walking up the hill to his home on Filbert. Richie had parked near Nolan's address, and as the Superior Savings Bank's data operations manager neared, he got out of his car and waited.

"Mr. Nolan?" Richie called.

Nolan stopped and cautiously eyed the man who'd spoken his name. Nolan was youthful looking, of medium height, with blond hair cut quite short, thick black-framed glasses, and wearing an inexpensive dark blue suit. As Richie stepped toward him, Nolan pushed his glasses higher up on his nose, and a glint of recognition filled his eyes. "Yes?"

"The name is Richard Amalfi. I'd like to talk to you."

"I know who you are. And I'm sorry, I have nothing to say to you." Nolan walked even faster towards his apartment.

Richie didn't give up. "I only have a few questions, and I can ask them here on the street if you'd like, but I would imagine it would be more comfortable and perhaps better for you if we spoke indoors, inside your apartment."

Nolan stopped in front of a six-story building. He used a key to unlock the main entrance door. As he stepped inside, he made no effort to stop Richie from following him. "I understand from Brian and Grant that you've already talked to them," he said as he pushed the elevator button. "They told me that they tried to answer your questions, but that they had nothing of particular interest or note to say to you. And I know I have even less. I had nothing to do with your fiancée, Mr. Amalfi. And for you to ask me questions or to insinuate that I was in any way involved with her or with her death, is simply a waste of your time, and an insult to me."

The elevator door opened. Richie stared at it. He hated elevators, always had, always would. There was something unnatural about willingly getting into a box that dangled in the air, held only by a thick cable. Richie got on, held his breath up to the sixth floor, and when the doors opened, he was the first one off.

Richie followed Nolan into a starkly modern apartment with a dark purple, armless sofa, two high-back black easy chairs, a wrought-iron-and-glass coffee table, matching end tables, and a big-screen TV that hung over a starkly modern fireplace.

"I guess you may as well ask your questions," Nolan said as he sat on the sofa and gestured toward a black chair for Richie.

"I know about the real estate holding company scheme that

Audrey Poole was involved in," Richie said. "But I don't know how much Isabella knew about it. It's obvious that she did find out something, something that got her killed. You, on the other hand, had to have known quite a bit about it since you oversaw the data input to your system."

"That's where you're wrong, Mr. Amalfi," Nolan said. "To me, it was nothing but API Holdings, LLC, one of a gazillion LLC's and corporations the bank handles. If there were such a scheme, and I'm not saying that there was or there wasn't, I would have had nothing whatsoever to do with it. My job is to make sure that the input from the local branch gets processed on time and accurately. And then, each morning when our branch opens its doors, I need to be sure all the prior day's information has been updated. I have nothing to do with real estate, fancy holding companies, or tax evasion schemes."

"How did the data from the real estate transactions get input to your data operations?" Richie asked.

"Inputs are made at the time the loan is taken by the staff that took in the forms and pieces of evidence," Nolan said. "At the time of Isabella Russo's death, the ones inputting such high-value account data would only have been Isabella herself, or her assistant."

"And who was her assistant back then?"

"Cory Egerton, of course. Why?" Nolan asked.

"API Holdings dealt with extremely large transactions," Richie said. "Surely someone in your department had to oversee them to make sure that everything ran smoothly."

"Do you have any idea how much money there is in the city?" Nolan asked. "It would be impossible to keep track of every account with large transactions."

"I know that the FBI is very interested in what happened to Audrey Poole's company," Richie said. He knew no such thing, but why not get Nolan to sweat? The data operations manager was too smug by half. "There's already a great deal of evidence that this might have involved some kind of racketeering. If so, your bank is going to be sucked into it. And you might be as well."

"I'd only be sucked in if I had done something wrong. And I haven't."

"For your sake, Ethan," Richie said, "I hope you're telling the truth."

∽

Rebecca used her lunch break to meet retired traffic investigative officer, Jim Taylor, at a coffee shop on Mission Street near the Hall of Justice.

The day before, after looking at the Isabella Russo accident file, she phoned Taylor and asked if he remembered a single-car accident that had resulted in the death of a young woman on Doyle Drive about four years earlier. He did, and agreed to meet with her at lunch to talk about it.

She was sitting at a table when Taylor walked in, and she immediately knew who he was. There was something about a cop, retired or not, that other law enforcement officers recognized. A constant wariness and awareness of their surroundings, and the way their eyes scanned every stranger who came into view. She smiled at him, and he smiled back a nod of mutual recognition.

He ordered a black coffee and a sandwich, and sat across from her at the table. After greeting each other and making small talk about the state of the Bureau of Inspections—who still worked there, who had retired, gotten promoted, and so forth—the time came for Rebecca to ask her questions.

"Something came up that caused me to look into the accident that took Isabella Russo's life," she began. "No one, yet, is thinking that the accident was anything other than an accident, but still, I'd like to hear your reaction to what you saw that morning. I realize it was a long time ago..."

"No problem," Taylor said. "I remember it well because it did bother me. It didn't make sense unless she fell asleep. It's possible, of course, but something didn't feel right. The way the car hit, the way the fenders were so banged up. I mean, anything can happen, but still..."

"And it was a fairly small car?" Rebecca added before taking a sip of her latte.

"Yeah," he said with a shake of the head as if he was remembering a few too many ugly accidents.

She gave him a moment, then said, "There had been a call shortly before the accident concerning two cars speeding along the parkway. I saw nothing in the file about those two cars. Did anyone attempt to follow-up on them?"

"Yeah, I did, but the caller didn't have any real information for us. Maybe I forgot to note that because it was a big nothing. Remember, it was still dark that time in the morning, and there was a thick fog. That made it hard to see the color or make of the cars involved. We looked at results from red light traffic cams to see if we could find anything. We did see a car, one car, that ran a red light just before the parkway. It turned out the car had been stolen. It was never retrieved. The whole thing added to my suspicions, but there isn't much that can be done with suspicion—not legally, anyway. Soon, we had no reason to continue the investigation, and it was ruled an accident."

"What about traffic cameras on the bridge?" Rebecca asked.

"Nothing suspicious. There were few cars heading north, but there are turnoffs before getting on the bridge itself. Besides, everyone took the accident as a tragic, single-car fatality. People were actually glad no one else was killed—as might have happened if the accident had occurred just a half-hour later in the morning."

Rebecca understood what he wasn't saying. This wasn't an

accident the higher-ups wanted to spend manpower, time, or money investigating. It was easy to mark "closed," and move onto the next one. One of the ironies in Traffic was that the two-car accidents where people survived and started suing anyone they could, took the majority of time to investigate. When it was a single car fatality, well, the dead don't complain.

"Did you talk to anyone who had an idea of where Isabella Russo was going at that time of the morning?" Rebecca asked.

Taylor took another bite of his sandwich and swallowed before answering. "After getting your call, I took a look at my notebook to refresh my memory. Some managers of the bank lived in Marin County, so she could have been going there, but none had any idea why. They were all shocked and nervous when talking to me. I didn't care for any of them, personally, but there was nothing I could put my finger on." He handed her a piece of paper. "I wrote down the names of the people who lived in Marin in case you want to talk to them."

"Thanks." She was grateful for his thoroughness. Clearly, the case had troubled him. She glanced at the names—Brian Skarzer, manager; Grant Yamada, assistant branch manager; Cory Egerton, assistant loan officer. She folded the paper and put it in her pocket. "What about things found in her car? Was there anything especially noteworthy or interesting?"

"All I remember were her handbag and laptop."

"She had a cell phone?"

"Yes. In her handbag."

"I guess you checked her phone, text messages, and emails to see if there was any explanation of where she was going and why?"

"We did. We found nothing."

"What about the laptop? Did you look at it to see if it had an explanation for her trip north?"

"Like I said, no one wanted to question what had happened to the woman. So, when they saw that the laptop was password protected, and no one had the password, it was put aside. We talked to her boss, but he said it wasn't the bank's. We looked a little into her personal life. Other than her fiancé being a bit sketchy, we saw no reason to think anyone wanted to harm her."

"Did we keep any of her things?"

"No. We gave everything back to her parents."

Rebecca nodded. "Okay, thanks. You've been a big help. If anything comes of this, I'll let you know."

"Good to hear. Some cases stick with you, as I'm sure you've learned, Rebecca. That one did," he said softly. "If I think of anything else, I'll give you a call."

12

Later that afternoon, Richie met Shay and Vito at one of Richie's favorite eateries, The Leaning Tower Taverna on Columbus Avenue in the North Beach district.

Shay and Vito were already seated at Richie's preferred booth in the far back of the diner when he arrived. The cafe's owner had been known to ask other patrons to leave the booth whenever Richie showed up unexpectedly.

The waitress followed Richie with his favorite beer in hand, Anchor Steam, and then waited patiently while he greeted his friends before ordering carbonara with prosciutto for lunch.

Shay had a cup of tea in front of him, while Vito was working on a beef tongue sandwich on a sourdough roll. Vito was Shay's opposite in every way, from his wide, ham-fisted build, to his grungy clothes, including the brown car coat he wore rain or shine, with bulging pockets so filled with junk they actually made Richie nervous that something might have died in there. And Shay would never have worn anything as garish as Vito's pancake-size wristwatch or chunky, solid gold pinky ring. Also, Vito was married with five children, while Shay was a consummate loner.

"What's Shay telling me, Richie?" Vito asked when the waitress had gone. "You gotta know you shouldn't go looking for no trouble. Isabella, may she rest in peace, needs to be left in peace!"

"I've got to check this out," Richie said. "You know me, Vito. How could I forgive myself if I didn't? I've already talked to the bank manager, assistant manager, and data operations manager. While I can't be sure that anyone of them had anything to do with Isabella's death, I can say that each looks guiltier than the other."

"What dicks," Vito grumbled.

"You got that right," Richie said.

"And it ain't no job I'd wanna do," Vito said, and the other two nodded in agreement.

"Anyway," Richie continued, "I've asked Shay to look into the bank's books. If anything is going on, that's where we'll find the evidence—but probably he's not going to find anything. Right, Shay?" He actually was hopeful that his prediction would be correct.

Shay continued to stir his tea, staring absently at the cup. His silence was uncomfortable. When he looked up, his expression was solemn. "There is a problem. You told Vito to keep an eye on Rebecca. But who's watching you?"

"Me? Why me?"

Shay looked to Vito to reply.

Vito looked more hangdog than ever as he explained, "Well, you see, I was talking to Carmela about you just this morning. You know how she always wants to keep tabs on you and she's worried about what's going on with you because of Isabella."

"Jesus! How did she find out...?" Richie didn't bother to finish his question. He knew Carmela routinely phoned Vito "just to say hello" and then grilled him about Richie's life. And no matter how much Vito tried to keep things from her,

Carmela knew how to get information out of him. "When will that woman realize I'm not a little kid anymore?"

"Probably never," Vito said honestly. "Anyway, she told me about a guy who showed up at her house and asked her questions about you. He said his company had some money to give you from an old investment that was finally paying off—a couple grand, in fact. But they didn't know how to reach you and needed an address. She wouldn't give it to him but she told him that he should be able to find you just about every evening down at Big Caesar's. She asked me if she did right. I told her she did."

"What a crazy ass story," Richie mumbled. "Did she say what the guy looked like?"

"Only that he was young and acted like he was just repeating words someone told him to say. She asked what company, but he said he didn't know. Sounded like some stooge someone sent to question Carmela."

Richie frowned. "How the hell did this guy find her? It doesn't make any sense."

"Well, she's in the phone book. Maybe he just called around. But whoever's behind it must've gone down to Big Caesar's because next thing I know, I'm watching the Inspector's apartment and when you showed up, I see a car trailing you. When you left, the car left. Maybe I shouldn't have done it, but I followed it. It went right up to your home, remained a while, and then split. I stopped following when they got on the Golden Gate Bridge approach and went back to the Inspector's place."

Vito described the car as a black Lexus SUV with tinted glass. He thought only one man was inside, but he couldn't be sure of that.

"Okay," Richie said. "Thanks, that's good to know. What about Rebecca? Does she seem safe?"

"Yeah. She seems fine. I just watched her have lunch with some guy."

Richie's eyebrows rose. "Someone she works with?"

"No, didn't seem to be. They looked like friends. He looked like a plain clothes cop, if you ask me. I'm sure she's safe with him. Anyway, they seemed to have a nice lunch, then she went back to work."

Richie grimaced. "A nice lunch. Great."

"What's the deal?" Shay asked Richie. "Why are you having Vito do this? In the past, whenever you've worried about Mayfield, you've looked after her yourself. Why not do that and free up Vito to watch your back?"

"Not this time," Richie said, simultaneously feeling guilty, stricken, and idiotic. "Not now."

Shay stared at him hard. "What do you mean, not now? Why not?"

"Nothing!"

Shay's eyes narrowed. "This doesn't have anything to do with you looking into what happened to Isabella, does it?"

That was a question he wasn't sure he could answer. He was saved from trying to when the waitress placed his lunch on the table in front of him.

He stared at the bowl of pasta, his appetite gone. He could feel Shay's questioning stare and continued to avoid him, at long last taking a bite. He chewed, but found it hard to swallow.

Shay leaned back in the booth, his arms crossed. "You've got to be kidding me."

"What?" Vito asked, confused, looking from Shay to Richie.

Richie scowled at Shay. "It's nothing, all right?" He faced Vito. "Nothing, got it?"

Vito gulped. "Sure, boss. Hey, I don't mind watching the Inspector. It's fine."

After a long silence, Shay said to Richie, "On a completely

different subject, have you heard if Rebecca identified the skeleton yet?"

"No, I haven't. As I said, I haven't seen or even talked to her much lately. Maybe I've stayed away too long," he added with a quick glance at Vito, then again faced Shay. "Why do you want to know?"

Shay shrugged. "No reason. I'm just curious about these new databases the police are using."

Richie nodded. He usually enjoyed being with his friends, but nothing was enjoyable these days.

He missed Rebecca. He missed their easy rapport, even when she challenged him. Missed the need to be constantly alert and vigilant around her. Missed her touch.

Hell, he missed everything about her.

∽

After spending the afternoon trying to find out more about Yussef Najjar with little success, Rebecca went to the shooting range for some practice, and afterward to the gym to work off some of the pent-up energy and anxiety she was feeling over the situation with Richie.

She simply didn't know how to deal with his issue. After talking to Jim Taylor, she could understand Richie's suspicions about Isabella's death. The chance was great that there was nothing to it—probably 80% that the death was an accident as had been determined—yet questions were unavoidable.

She had returned home, showered, and was trying to decide if she was hungry enough to cook up some dinner, when she heard a knock on her apartment door.

Kiki, she thought. The idea of seeing her friend, who would probably want to head out somewhere to eat, was a welcome one. She swung open the door.

It was Richie. She wanted to wrap her arms around him,

but thoughts of all she had learned about his former fiancée stopped her. She stood there gawking at him for far too long and then invited him in.

His expression was grim. Instead of kissing her or greeting Spike—things he usually did when he walked into her home—he said only, "We've got to talk." And then he began to pace.

"All right." Nervous, she went over to the sofa and sat. Spike perched at her side, and as Richie walked back and forth, their eyes followed his steps, their heads all but synchronized. The room was so small, he could only take a few steps before he needed to turn around and go the other way.

Finally he spoke. "The more I've thought about it, the more concerned I've become about your safety."

That was *not* what she expected to hear. "What in the world are you talking about?"

"You know very well what I mean. You know you're in danger." He stopped and faced her, then ran a hand over the back of his head, a sure sign of anxiety with him.

"Are you talking about that sniper? That was weeks ago!"

"Yes, and just last week you were left warning notes on your car and on your front door, and earlier this week, a truck could have killed you. Maybe even *tried* to kill you."

"How do you know about that?"

"That doesn't matter!" He was waving his arms now. "I think it's all connected. You've got a target on your back."

"Don't be—"

"Stop! Just get your things, and Spike's, and come stay at my place until we find out what's going on." He clamped his mouth shut and waited for her answer.

She drew in her breath, then softly, calmly stated, "You can't be serious."

"I'm beyond serious," he said, practically seething.

She got up, went to the kitchen, took out two stemmed

glasses and poured them each a glass of claret. "Richie, sit down."

He didn't sit, but she handed him his glass anyway as she returned to the sofa. "Yes, something happened. Yes, I was in danger. But I'm being careful, and watchful. If I get any idea I'm in danger again, I'll go to your place and hide. Okay?"

He put the wine on the coffee table and continued pacing. "No, it's not okay. It's not enough." With an exasperated sigh, he dropped onto the sofa beside her, and put his hands on her arms, facing her squarely. "I'd like you to move in with me."

"I said that when, or if—"

"Permanently."

Her breath caught, then she put down her glass as well. There were times she'd been crazy enough to be ready to follow him anywhere, but this wasn't one of them. It took a moment before she found her voice. "Now, I know you're joking."

"I've never been more serious."

She couldn't help but wish his words were true. She suspected he believed they were, but she also suspected, no, she *knew*, there was more to it.

His hands felt warm on her arms, and his gaze was too deep, too caring, for her to say what she needed to. The subject had been on her mind for a few days, and this was—unfortunately—the time to bring it up.

Much as she hated to.

She broke his hold and walked to the kitchen. With both hands flat on the counter, she took a deep breath before she turned to face him again. The confusion, even the hurt, in his eyes tore at her. Her mouth felt dry. "Richie, I know that you've been looking into Isabella's death."

"How—?"

She put up her hand and shook her head, stopping him from asking. "I understand that, given what happened to her, you're afraid something will happen to me as well. But you can't keep me in bubble-wrap at your house. That's not who I am."

"You think I'm projecting her onto you? Not in the least! You two couldn't be more different. I'm worried about you. Only about you." His gaze was so intense it rocked her.

She was so, so tempted to take him up on his offer. She needed to get the conversation away from her, and she could think of one sure way to do it. She folded her arms, all but hugging herself against the waves of emotion emanating from him. "Did you ever figure out where Isabella was going that morning?"

He looked shocked by the question. "How do you know it was an issue?"

"I looked at the accident file. It hung like a huge question mark over the whole case. That, and a call someone made to nine-one-one saying two cars were speeding on the bridge approach."

"What call?" he asked, the color gone from his face.

"You hadn't heard?" That surprised her, and by his reaction, she knew he hadn't. "It might not have had anything to do with her accident—or had everything to do with it. Two cars were apparently seen speeding along the Marina Green heading for the tunnel to the bridge. The call was made only about ten minutes before another call reporting the accident." She paused. "The fog was so heavy that morning, no one was able to clearly see what was going on."

He swallowed hard. "Yes, I remember that fog. It still blanketed everything after I got the call from her parents and drove out to spot where the accident took place. I wanted—needed—to see what had happened, but it had been all cleared up. Can't inconvenience the commuters, after all." He stopped talking as memories hit. "No one said anything about another car, or cars, or a nine-one-one call."

"There wasn't much to it. Not enough information to follow-up."

He steepled his hands, his eyes bleak. His breathing came fast, too fast. "So Isabella might have been out there with some other driver—someone she was trying to get away from. That means she might have known, tried to get away, that she was scared, so damned scared…"

"No." Rebecca sat beside him, wishing that she could make it right for him, but that was beyond anyone's ability. She lightly rubbed his shoulder. "We don't know that. The speeders could have been long gone before Isabella ever reached the area. We don't know how much time passed between the person seeing the speeders and reporting them. When pressed for information—type of car, license, etc.—he said he didn't know because of the fog, and then hung up. No one investigated beyond looking at traffic cams and seeing nothing."

"Except that there were few skid marks," he murmured.

So, she thought, the police told him that much—probably to help make the case Isabella most likely fell asleep at the wheel. She folded her hands on her lap. "The report could have been about anyone, even a couple of kids deciding to drag-race through the tunnel thinking it was empty."

"At six in the morning? I doubt it."

Good point, Rebecca thought. "We have no idea what happened, Richie."

Richie nodded. "Yeah, so I heard."

More than anything, she wished she hadn't brought this up. It was too personal, too raw. Perhaps it always would be. She hurt to see him this way.

"Stay for dinner," she said, trying to sound "normal" as she headed for the kitchen, knowing full well that normal might never be theirs again. "I went grocery shopping today and bought some steaks and potatoes. While I cook, try to relax, at least a little. You look exhausted."

She went into the kitchen, took the steaks out of the refrigerator, and placed them on the counter. She turned to smile at him, happy they were together again, even though the tension in the air was trying to keep them apart. She hoped to see his irrepressible smile, his mesmerizing gaze following her every move, but she saw none of that. He sat on the sofa, his head bowed. She ached to see him that way. "I'm so sorry, Richie. I truly am," she said softly. "I shouldn't have looked at the files. It wasn't my business. I thought I was helping, and all I've done is made you feel worse. I—"

"No! Stop, Rebecca." In an instant, he stood before her, his dark gaze capturing hers. "It's okay," he whispered. "You're a detective. Investigating is what you do."

She appreciated his words, but his understanding only made her feel worse. "I didn't mean to stick my nose in where it doesn't belong. I feel so bad."

He put his arms around her. "I probably would have asked you to read the file one of these days, anyway, especially if Shay's investigation into Superior Savings Bank turns up anything questionable."

She took a deep breath, gripping his shoulders. Then she lifted her hands to his head, her fingers stroking the gentle waves of his soft, ink-black hair. "I care about you, Richie," she whispered. "So very much."

"I know you do." He kissed her temple, the tip of her nose, and when his lips captured hers, the tension between them withered away.

She had no idea how long they stood there, caught up in a kiss she wasn't sure she ever wanted to end, but slowly she pulled back, still locked in his embrace. "Hungry?" she asked.

"Are you?"

"In more ways than one." She smiled. "But for now, let's cook."

He nodded and swung open a lower cabinet door to get a

frying pan. But then he stopped and regarded her with a knowing gaze.

She was puzzled. "Now what?"

"You don't normally go out and buy steaks for yourself for dinner. So this means you were thinking about me being here with you. Much as you say you don't see us working out as a couple, Rebecca, your actions speak a lot louder than your words."

She gave a slight nod, admitting everything he said was true.

"And, as for the invitation to move in with me, it still stands."

She raised her eyebrows.

"In fact," he took the steaks from the counter, put them back into the refrigerator, and took her in his arms again, "those will make a fine dessert, but I've got a much better idea about our main course."

13

Even after insistent urging, including bribes of foot and back massages whenever her heart desired, Rebecca refused to move into Richie's home. Still, they spent the weekend together. Something told her—a warning almost—not to let this moment slip through her fingers, to allow herself one weekend at least, a carefree and, yes, a romantic time. A calm before the storm, perhaps. But for once, she listened to her heart.

She found every moment filled with joy, once they put aside fruitless discussions of Isabella's accident or potential dangers to Rebecca. Of course, the topics were on both their minds, but she needed to simply enjoy the beauty of the world around her, and not dwell on its ugliness. And so did Richie.

On Sunday, they walked around Fisherman's Wharf, and when Richie learned Rebecca had never taken a boat tour of the bay, he whisked her onto one. They held hands as wind whipped through their hair. They stole kisses when no one was looking, and even when others were watching. They laughed at the antics of sea lions basking in the sun, and at nothing at all.

A part of her wondered if she wasn't being foolish not

taking Richie up on his offer to move in with him. But that was a commitment she wasn't sure she was ready to make, particularly since she felt he wouldn't have asked her if he wasn't worried about her being in danger. If she were to live with him, it had to be for a far better reason than a haunted sense of protectiveness.

On Monday morning, she walked into work wearing her best poker face. If she came in happy from her weekend, the teasing from her fellow detectives would have been merciless.

She hadn't even finished her morning coffee before she received a call from Patti Flynn, her State Department contact. Flynn could find no information that Yussef Najjar had traveled to Lebanon. That wasn't to say he hadn't traveled there using a fake identification of some sort, which was becoming increasingly common when dealing with certain Middle Eastern countries. All she could attest to was that Najjar hadn't traveled under his own name.

Flynn had continued to look into the matter, however, and called up information about the family. Some twenty-eight years earlier, at age fifteen, Yussef Najjar entered the US with his mother, Fairuz, and an older brother, Gebran. They had gained admittance to the US through the Fairuz's brother, who petitioned the government to bring his widowed sister and her two teenage sons into the country. Flynn had a San Francisco address for Gebran and Fairuz Najjar.

Rebecca gave Sutter the information, and the two decided it was time to pay a visit to give Yussef's relatives the bad news— and to see if one of them might not be the prime suspect in Yussef's murder.

Rebecca was about to leave the office with Sutter when a call came into her from Jim Taylor, the retired traffic investigator. He was calling to say he had remembered something that had struck him as strange at the time. A few months after the accident, he had contacted the bank to finish up a few loose ends before he sent the folder off to be filed. To his surprise, the man who had been Isabella's assistant, Cory Egerton, no longer work there. His coworkers hadn't been able to reach him by phone or email. A woman in the office said she'd dropped by his apartment, only to find that he'd moved and left no forwarding address. Taylor had tried to locate him, but without luck. Eventually, he gave up and simply filed away the case.

∽

Richie drove into Ross Alley and parked in one of his favorite places—the red zone in front of Canton Souvenirs, a wholesale supplier of tourist kitsch. Since street parking was essentially nonexistent in Chinatown, the owner of the warehouse had had the curb painted red but he allowed his friends to use the space for short visits to the area. Others who parked there found their cars towed away almost immediately. Richie's car never was.

From Ross Alley, Richie walked a block to the Five Families Association, and asked to speak to Milton Jang, its current head.

He was shown to Jang's office. Jang placed his cigarette and its holder on an ashtray as he rose from his desk chair, one hand outstretched to shake Richie's. He had a slight but steely build, with withered skin and dyed black hair. "Ah, my friend. To what do I owe this honor?"

Richie grinned. Jang always spoke that way, knowing Richie was the one who should feel honored to have been let in to see him so quickly. "The honor is mine," Richie said, playing his role in the ritual as their hands met.

Jang smirked and walked over to some comfortable chairs, gesturing for Richie to take one of them as he poured them each a snifter of brandy.

Richie was always amazed by the beauty of Jang's office.

The ceiling was carved teak, the walls mostly filled with scrolls and paintings, while étagères housed porcelains and vases from long-ago dynasties. In addition, the room's carved wooden furniture pieces had been made in San Francisco's Chinatown, and the gold display pieces all came from the California Gold Rush of 1849 that brought the first Chinese immigrants to "Gold Mountain," as they called their new home.

"I hear your nightclub is doing very well." Jang placed the brandy on a small table between them and sat.

"You should come see it," Richie said, "as my guest. Bring friends and family, as many as you'd like."

"Perhaps one day, although I rarely leave my home and office."

"I can see why." Richie looked over the room with a nod of admiration.

"So, what brings you here when you should be out with that lovely homicide detective I'm told you are seeing?" Jang asked.

"She's the reason I'm here," Richie said. "You have influence in city politics."

"Who, me?" Jang said with a big smile.

"Oh, how could I forget? You never get involved in anything that isn't saintly," Richie said. "Let's cut the bull. This is serious—like, life and death serious."

Jang's eyebrows rose with interest. "Go on."

Richie explained why he thought someone in city government had been involved in phony real estate deals, and Rebecca had gotten dangerously close to uncovering it.

Jang nodded. "Crooked money, crooked politicians. What else is new? So, why are you here?"

"Because I'm hoping you know the people involved."

"I had nothing to do with any of that," Jang insisted.

"I agree," Richie said. "But you know many of the people involved in this kind of business. I need names."

Jang smirked. "Sometimes my memory is not good."

Richie's expression hardened. "If we were just talking about money and screwy real estate deals, I wouldn't give a damn either. Who the hell cares? We've worked together and did pretty well more than once. But this is different. There's a lot more going on—and whatever it is has put Inspector Mayfield in danger. It's centered in city government. The mayor's chief of staff didn't commit suicide. He was murdered."

Jang sat back in his chair and stared at Richie. "Those are strong words, my friend. You must be careful where you say things like that, or you might find you're committing suicide just like the mayor's chief of staff did."

"I'm here asking you to help," Richie said.

"Why should I get involved at all? For the good of the city, or my conscience?"

"No. For power." Richie leaned forward. "If you have the power to take down the guys who are behind this in the city government, you'll be the one running the city. Not openly, but everyone who matters will know what happened, and know where the real power in the city lies. I believe you would very much enjoy being in that position."

Jang's black eyes stared at him, then slowly crinkled into a smile. "I believe you are quite correct. I will look into this situation. I could not allow the future Mrs. Amalfi to be placed in danger, could I?"

Richie swallowed. "I wouldn't say there'll be a future Mrs. Amalfi anytime soon—and probably not the inspector unless she has a major change of heart about yours truly. But all that aside, I'll be grateful for anything you can do to help, and under an obligation to help you in the future in any way I can."

Jang smiled, then nodded slowly. "Keep sending profitable business my way. That's payment enough. For now."

14

Rebecca and Bill Sutter rang the doorbell of the Najjar home on Lobos Street in the Oceanview area, a once crime-infested area that was now making a comeback due to the ever increasing cost of property in the city. One of the more curious aspects of the Oceanview area was that it had no view at all of the ocean, being inland and at the city's southernmost edge.

It was evening. The two detectives had purposely waited until 7:30 p.m. in hopes of finding Gebran Najjar, the brother of the deceased, at home. They had investigated him a bit and learned he owned a dry cleaning business in the area. He'd had it for fifteen years. He and his wife were buying the house they lived in. His mother, Fairuz, also lived there.

From inside the house they heard children calling their mother, and a girl's voice asking if she could open the door.

"Go! I'll get it," a woman shouted back just before the door swung open.

Rebecca stared at an attractive woman, probably in her late thirties, with dark brown eyes, olive skin, and thick black hair that fell past her shoulders. "Yes?" she asked. The mouthwatering scent of spicy cooking wafted out to Rebecca, and she hoped her stomach didn't growl with hunger.

"We are looking for Gebran Najjar," Rebecca said. "Does he live here?"

"Yes. He is my husband." The woman's dark eyes looked hesitant and worried. She spoke with a slight accent.

Rebecca and Sutter introduced themselves, showing their badges. "Is he home?" Rebecca asked.

"Yes. We were just about to sit down to dinner." The woman frowned at those words, as if realizing a couple of detectives appearing at the door took precedence over sitting down to a meal. "Please come in. I'll call him."

"Thank you," Rebecca said. "Your name is?"

"Salma Najjar."

They walked up the stairs to the main living quarters of the home, and Salma Najjar showed them to the living room. Two children, a boy, about eleven or twelve, and a younger girl were there.

"Go to your rooms and be quiet," Salma ordered. The two hurried away with barely a backward glance.

She gestured toward the sofa. "Have a seat," she said to the detectives.

A large, burly man with dark eyes, a balding head, and deeply tanned skin entered the room. He wore gray slacks, and a white undershirt, as if he had taken off whatever dress shirt he might have been wearing. On his feet were slippers.

"Who are our guests?" he asked.

"This is my husband," Salma said softly. He looked a good ten years older than his wife, and like her, his accent was practically nonexistent.

Rebecca and Sutter rose to their feet as they introduced themselves.

"We're here with news about Yussef Najjar," Sutter said. "We understand he's your brother?"

"That is correct," Gebran said. He and Salma glanced at each other and she inched closer to him.

"Is your mother here with you?" Rebecca asked.

"No, she is not." Gebran glanced briefly at Rebecca, then fixed his gaze on Sutter. "What do you know about Yussef?"

Rebecca gave Sutter a slight nod, and he said, "I'm sorry to inform you that his body has been found."

Gebran stiffened. "He is dead?"

"Yes. It's clear he has been dead at least nine years, most likely from the time he was first reported missing."

"Where did you find him?" Gebran's words were gruff.

"Please," Rebecca said, interrupting. "Let's all sit down. This is a shock, I'm sure."

As they sat, Sutter went on to explain, as delicately as he could, the circumstances of the discovery.

"We are looking into the reasons for his death," Rebecca said. "But first, we have one question. When the Missing Persons investigators were looking into his disappearance, his mother told them he had gone back to Lebanon. We find, now, there is no evidence of that."

Gebran rubbed the palm of one hand hard against his knee. "I remember those days. They were very upsetting. Our mother also told us that my brother had returned to Lebanon. We didn't question her about it. Many problems are going on in that country. If Yussef went back there, we didn't want to know why, or to have anything more to do with him."

Rebecca wondered about his answer. "Is that because he might have gotten involved in the country's politics?"

"No, no. We stay out of politics and the wars. We are Christians," Gebran stated firmly.

"We go to Our Lady of Lebanon," Salma added softly.

Rebecca glanced at Sutter, eyebrows raised. He shook his head. Neither had heard of such a church.

Gebran added, "It's in Millbrae, the only Maronite Catholic

Church in the area." Millbrae was on the peninsula between San Francisco and San Mateo where Yussef had worked and lived. Gebran then scowled at Salma, as if she should know better than to speak. The room filled with tension.

"Tell me a little about yourselves," Rebecca said. "Do you work?"

Gebran told her about his dry-cleaning business, confirming her research. She faced Salma. "And you? Do you have a job?"

She looked stricken. "No. I help my husband when he needs me. And I do the books and pay bills for his business. That's all."

Rebecca faced Gebran. "Did you ever employ your brother?"

"No." The word was sharply spoken.

"Do you have other employees?" Sutter asked.

"Only my wife's father. He doesn't speak good English, so he works in the back. I handle the customers."

Sutter nodded. "And his name is?"

"Zair Lahoud, but he knows nothing about all this. And what does my business have to do with my brother's death?"

"You tell me," Sutter said. "Why didn't anyone go back to the police when you found out your brother wasn't in Lebanon?"

"I didn't know," Gebran said. "I only knew what my mother told me. My brother and I weren't close."

"Was he younger or older?" Rebecca asked.

"Younger. Two years." Gebran stared at the floor as he answered.

"Married?" Rebecca asked once more.

"No."

"Did he have a girlfriend or a partner?" she asked.

His eyes flashed angrily. "You ask if he's gay?"

"I'm asking you about others who might have been close to

him." Rebecca did her best to keep her voice calm and friendly. "The only leads in his file were people he worked with and this family."

"No one was close to him but us," Gebran said.

Salma seemed to shrink further and further into herself with each outburst.

"We would like to speak to your mother," Rebecca said. "We understand she lives here. Will she return home soon?"

"She is in a nursing home. She has some dementia and my wife could not care for her," Gebran said.

"Which one?" Sutter asked.

"Let me talk to her doctor first." Gebran's voice grew colder, harder, with each word. "To give her such news about her son, in her condition ... I want to be sure she can handle it."

Rebecca and Sutter glanced at each other. "That's fine. We'll call you in a day or so to find out what arrangements have been made for us to speak with her," Sutter said.

Gebran nodded, and then he asked, "Tell me, do you have any idea what caused my brother's death?"

"It appears he was shot," Sutter said. "We don't yet have any idea why, but we've retrieved the bullet. We'll figure it out."

Salma put her hands to her mouth, her eyes wide as she looked at her husband with something close to horror.

Gebran's reaction was the opposite. He lifted his chin and gave a firm nod. "It sounds like a robbery. This used to be a bad area, people shot for no reason. It's gotten much better lately."

"But his body was found far from this area," Rebecca pointed out.

Gebran shrugged. "Who can explain what killers do?"

"One thing, still, is not clear," Rebecca said. "Why did your mother say her son had left the country when he hadn't?"

"I have no idea." Gebran's lips curled in disgust. "I'm sure she believed it."

"And what about you, Mrs. Najjar?" Rebecca asked. "Do you have any idea why his mother said he had gone to Lebanon?"

Salma looked scared, whether because of the question or simply because she was being directly questioned, Rebecca had no idea. Salma gazed at her husband. He nodded.

"I have no idea," she began, then cleared her throat, "why my mother-in-law said what she did."

Rebecca hadn't really expected anything else. Time to leave.

As she walked out of the living room, Rebecca saw the two children scramble from the hallway into a bedroom, and then quietly shut the door.

∽

Since the hour was late, Rebecca and Sutter had each driven their own cars to the Najjar home. When they left, Rebecca waved goodbye to Sutter, saying she would see him in the morning.

She got into her Ford Explorer and headed toward home. She had only gone about a half mile when, stopped for a red light, she was thrown into her steering wheel and heard the crunch of her back bumper. "What the hell!" she grumbled, one hand flying to her ribs. The sudden jolt rattled her, but thankfully she wasn't hurt.

She grabbed her car registration and her handbag and got out of the SUV.

The car behind her was an old two-tone Lincoln Continental. She was surprised that the driver hadn't gotten out yet, especially since it looked as if his front bumper had sustained more damage than her back one. Still, it was enough damage that she was plenty pissed off.

She stood, arms crossed, glaring at her bumper as the Lincoln's door opened, and a man stepped out. He didn't exactly look like a Wall Street type. His expression was gruff, his build burly, and his face pockmarked and deeply tanned. As he stepped past the door, she saw that he held a handgun, and it was pointed at her.

"What's this?" she asked, the picture of calm. She'd be damned if she'd let the man scare her.

"Drop the purse, lady." The stranger held the gun as if he knew how to use it.

"You don't want to mess with me," she said as she placed her handbag on the street, then took a step back. "What's going on?"

"I know who you are," he replied. "Now, remove the gun you're wearing."

The words surprised her. He knew she was a cop. "I'm not. It's in my handbag."

He looked pleased. "You better be telling me the truth. Just sayin'. I see any sudden move, and I shoot. Take that as a warning, Inspector. Now, get in the car."

"Not a chance."

"You heard me! Get in!" He waved the gun toward the Lincoln so there was no mistake about his order. She needed to stay calm and cool, but she felt her legs weakening.

The creep stopped waving the gun and thrust it toward her. His sneer proved that he wouldn't hesitate using it if she didn't do as he said.

She took a first step toward the Lincoln, thinking about her next strategic move, but before she could take a second step, a large gray Dodge Ram pickup sped down the street, heading straight at them.

"Look out!" Rebecca shouted.

The gunman's head jerked around at the roar of the truck's engine heading his way. Seeing it closing in on him, he ran toward the sidewalk and dived out of the way with barely a second to spare.

Through the windshield, Rebecca could see Vito behind

the truck's wheel. He swerved to avoid Rebecca, and then stomped on the brake. "Let's go!" he shouted through the open window.

She only paused long enough to grab her handbag, then jumped in the passenger side. He was speeding away before she even shut the door.

"We'll go back and pick up your car once we know it's safe," Vito said. "Or I'll give Shay a call and have him get it and deliver it to your house. That way, for sure, there'll be no danger to you."

She was shaking from fear and adrenaline as she murmured, "What are you doing here?" The words were no sooner out of her mouth than she realized exactly what he was doing there. "No need to answer that." She took a few deep breaths before adding, "Just tell Richie, it seems he's right. This time."

15

Rebecca had to admit that after the prior evening's attack, she took Richie's paranoia over her well-being a lot more seriously than she had previously.

As much as she preferred to be logical and practical, her gut cried out that things were not as they should be at work, and that the problem might start higher up on the food chain than her boss, Lieutenant James Philip Eastwood. All the way up to City Hall, in fact.

Calderon and Benson had been in charge of the investigation into the death of the Mayor's chief of staff, Sean Hinkle. But they had been pressured to end the investigation quickly, and that meant a determination of suicide. Lt. Eastwood had made it clear that if they delayed, they would not be looked upon with favor by anyone in the department or City Hall.

Normally, Calderon and Benson would have ignored Eastwood. Neither was the type that accepted attempts at intimidation with anything but scorn. In this case, however, they couldn't find anything to question. In fact, the main thing they questioned was Sean Hinkle's home. Nothing was out of order, and not a spot was found anywhere ... not even fingerprints. It had been wiped clean.

Rebecca decided to take a look at some of the findings herself. Calderon and Benson hadn't known Hinkle. She had. And dating him a couple of times had been one of her bigger lapses in judgment.

Once more, she found herself in the Records Division going through files until she found the one on Hinkle's death. The case had been closed, so the investigation materials had been sent there for storage. Since it was determined to have been a suicide, it didn't even warrant a "box" of material from the investigation, only a manila folder filled with Q's and A's of people who knew, worked with, or lived near Hinkle at the time of his death. His grieving parents were both alive, as well as a married sister. No one spoken to had any idea why he would kill himself. At the same time, the investigation turned up no reason for anyone to want him dead.

Rebecca turned to his financial records. His finances were in even worse shape than she had expected. He had even managed to lose money investing in API Holdings—the same holding company that Isabella Russo may have been working with at the time she died.

Suddenly, the call Rebecca had received from Jim Taylor came back to her with renewed significance. Isabella's assistant had quit his job and disappeared. The bank's personnel office should have had some record of where he might have gone, after all they had to send him his paycheck, tax reporting forms, all kinds of things. Taylor had said the man had left no forwarding address, but it was worth checking again.

Something told her that they might not cooperate if she merely called them on the phone. Paying them a visit in person, waving her badge, might go further to get the information she needed.

She quickly made copies of some of the information about

Sean Hinkle's finances and his arrangements with the real estate holding company, and stuck them in her bag.

Then, she phoned Richie.

∽

Rebecca always enjoyed going to Richie's house on a small street near the top of Twin Peaks in the center of the city. The style of the house was contemporary, with the garage and storerooms taking up the ground floor, and the living area above them. A long staircase led from the sidewalk to the front door, and a large picture window dominated the front of the house, giving Richie a beautiful view from his living room of the city below.

She pulled onto the driveway and walked up to the front door. When Richie opened it, he gave her a quick kiss. "Shay is here," he said, by way of explanation. In Richie's world, emotional displays with girlfriends weren't done in front of buddies. "You okay?" His eyes were worried.

"I'm fine," she said as she entered the living room. It was a sedate room, casual yet elegant, with a light gray sectional, two sky blue chairs, and tables in a pale ash—not to mention a 60-inch plasma TV. On one side of the room was a fireplace, and on the other, the picture window. Through it, the lights of the city shone like stars far below them.

She faced Shay and offered him a smile. "Thank you for bringing my car back last night."

Ever the gentleman, Shay stood. Not only did he dress like an aristocrat with wool slacks and soft handmade cotton shirts, but his manners reflected a formal upbringing as well. "No problem. Glad to be of service."

The fireplace had been lit, and George Gershwin's "Catfish Row" played softly on the stereo. The men were drinking beer—even Shay. Richie poured her a glass of chardonnay.

As they sat, she removed a copy of Sean Hinkle's file from her tote bag and handed it to Shay. "I'm sure Richie told you about the situation with the mayor's chief of staff's supposed suicide," she said. At Shay's nod, she continued. "Interviews with people who knew Hinkle are here, but more importantly, I've included papers about the real estate holding company he was once involved in. I believe there's a lot more to the holding company than we know, but when I look at this, I see a bunch of numbers that mean nothing. I'm hoping you can make sense of them."

Shay took the folder and flipped through the papers. He glanced at Richie. "These just might help in the other issue I was looking into."

"No need to keep it quiet," Richie said. "She found out I'm having you investigate Isabella's bank."

Shay looked surprised, but said nothing.

Richie turned to Rebecca. "Shay has already discovered that the bank wiped Audrey Poole's API Holdings account from their records. He's trying to find where it went, and who removed it. He'll also try, to the extent possible, to reconstruct what it looked like at the time Isabella was working on the real estate loans. We're wondering if anything might have jumped out at her as proof of wrong-doings, and if that isn't what caused ... well, if that didn't put her in danger."

"I'm not yet sure," Shay said, "that I'll have enough data to do it."

As she listened to all this, Rebecca couldn't help but think about Isabella's laptop. She hated to bring it up, but finally she said, "I suppose at the time of her death, there would have been no reason for Shay to try to get into her computer, but what about now?"

"It wouldn't help," Richie said. "She rarely used it, and definitely not for work. The bank had rules about security. Besides, she never even bothered with a password. I took a look, but it was more of a dust-collector than anything."

"That's surprising," Rebecca said. "I mean, if it was so unimportant, why did she have it with her at the time of the accident?"

"She didn't." Richie shook his head, as if not wanting to think about such things. "It was at her parents' house. In her room there."

Something didn't add up, Rebecca thought. "The investigator told me she had a laptop with her when she died. He couldn't get past the password, but since the accident apparently had no mitigating circumstances, he had no reason to pursue it further."

Richie's brows crossed. "I never heard she had a laptop with her. It wasn't hers. Are you sure?"

"I'm just repeating what I was told."

"Where is this laptop?" Shay asked.

"I believe it was returned to her parents. The bank's manager said it didn't belong to the bank."

"They may still have it," Richie whispered. He rubbed his jaw, deep in thought. "Damn!"

Rebecca saw the sadness in his expression and realized how hard it would be for him to face Isabella's family. "Would you like me to talk to them? If they still have it, I could say something has come up, that the SFPD just needs to borrow the laptop a short while."

He shook his head. "No. I should do it. I really should visit them anyway."

Rebecca glanced at Shay who gave a slight shake of the head. Then, in a much more optimistic voice than the situation warranted, she said, "I'm sure, if it exists, once Shay has it he'll be able to get into it and see exactly what was going on."

"I agree." Shay's voice also had a sudden unnatural lilt, as if he, too, was trying to lift Richie's spirits. "We'll find out what's going on."

"That's right," Rebecca said enthusiastically.

"Knock it off, you two," Richie said, shaking his head. "I can handle it."

"Good. I should get going," Shay said. "Oh, by the way, Rebecca. Any news on that skeleton of yours?"

She smiled. "Yes. We identified it."

Shay's mouth gaped a moment before he shut it and eased his demeanor back to the casual manner he usually displayed. "Oh?"

"He was an immigrant—Lebanese. Apparently his mother brought him here when he was young to get him away from the dangers in Lebanon. It's ironic that he ended up a murder victim."

Shay's coloring seemed to pale a bit. "Yes. What a surprising ending to the discovery."

"It's not quite ended yet," Rebecca said. "Now we have to figure out who killed him."

16

It was early. Shay rarely was awake at seven in the morning, let alone out and about. But after talking to Rebecca the night before, he couldn't sleep.

Now, Mrs. Brannigan gawked at him in complete shock as he put on a warm ascot and jacket and headed out the door before having his morning tea, let alone the hard-boiled egg and toast with lemon curd that made up his usual breakfast.

He headed down to the garage and got into his Maserati.

He might have told himself he planned to simply drive around, but he knew exactly where he was going—the Oceanview district.

He was relieved that all appeared to be quiet at the house. He could only hope everyone inside was calm, maybe even happy. The calm before the storm, as the saying went.

He took a deep breath as he stared at another man's home, knowing that inside, was another man's family.

His thoughts rarely strayed in such a direction. He was usually too much in control to allow that to happen. He again breathed deeply as he focused his mind toward emptiness, as if meditating. After a few moments, he felt settled, almost peaceful.

Seeing that all was well here, so far at least, he was about to start his car to leave when he saw a little girl and boy emerge from the house, and behind them a tall woman with long black hair pulled back in a barrette. She wore jeans, a pink shirt with long sleeves, and a warm-looking vest. He scarcely needed to look at her face, so etched was it in his memory, but he did.

She was as beautiful as ever, even in the early morning, even without make-up and still looking a little sleepy.

She handed the girl a lunch box, and the two turned in the direction in which he was parked. He recognized the boy, Adam, despite how much he'd grown. He would be about eleven or twelve now. Adam ran ahead of them down the block.

Shay thought about driving off, but that would surely get the woman's attention. Instead, he reached for the baseball cap he kept in the car to cover his blond hair when he was on surveillance. And then, to be extra cautious, he put on sunglasses even though it wasn't a particularly sunny morning.

The girl walked along the outer edge of the sidewalk, closest to his car.

His eyes couldn't leave the child. Her hair was fine and straight and a light brown color. And as she walked past the car, she looked into it and her eyes met his. He lowered the sunglasses just a bit, enough to be sure of what he was seeing. Her irises were large and pale blue, with a hint of lavender around the edges.

As quickly as she had faced him, she turned her attention back to the sidewalk and continued on her way, her mother at her side.

The girl was, if he could be completely objective, a somewhat odd-looking child, with light olive skin in eyes so large and pale they dominated her face—a face that held a curious yet intelligent expression as she gazed back at him.

But there was nothing objective in his heart as he looked at her. He was too familiar with the countenance he saw before him.

He hadn't known how quickly and completely emotion could strike—a bizarre mixture that made him feel both protective and filled with awe. He hadn't known such a feeling, ever. Not until he looked at that child and recognized the features he saw in his mirror each day.

He could scarcely breathe.

At the corner, a school bus came by and stopped.

When it pulled away again, the girl and boy were no more to be seen, and the woman stood still and watched it.

Before she turned back toward her house, he drove away.

~

Richie opened the door of his home to find his mother, Carmela, standing before him with a massive, covered casserole in her hand.

"Richie, I brought you some manicotti, your favorite," Carmela said. She was a short woman, stout, with copper-colored hair so stiff from hairspray it looked like a helmet.

"What's this?" Richie asked as he stepped aside to let Carmela enter.

She faced him, her eyes troubled. "I heard you've been looking into what happened to Isabella," Carmela said. "I'm worried about you, Richie."

"Vito talks too much," Richie mumbled.

"He's a good friend! He worries about you so he talks to me." Carmela shouted the words, raising her arms toward Heaven. "And I worry, too!"

"Yeah, well, Vito's got to learn to mind his own business!" Richie shouted right back, in true Italian family style. He walked into the kitchen and Carmela followed. She put the manicotti onto the counter.

"Is it cooked?" Richie asked, trying to calm down. What was it about mothers? Or was it just the Italian ones, he wondered. "Or do I need to cook it?"

Carmela harrumphed, hands on hips. "You can't take my attention away from this. But, you will need to cook it—three-fifty, about ninety minutes. Anyway, I know how horrible it was for you and all of us when we lost Isabella. I don't want you to bring all that back again." When Richie didn't respond, she waggled her finger at him, her voice even louder. "You understand what I'm saying to you?!"

"Yes, Ma," he said softly, as he made room in his refrigerator for the casserole, then made them both a cup of coffee. Carmela always enjoyed having a cup and sitting down at the kitchen table talking to him. It was the sort of thing they had done over most of his life, usually at her house. Whenever things got bad, Carmela would serve coffee with cookies or other Italian pastry that she might have made or bought, and they'd sit in the kitchen and have a heart-to-heart. It was one of the things that came from Richie having been an only child and losing his father when he was only five years old.

"I found out some things about Isabella's death," Richie said, "and I need to look into it. I can't let it go, not knowing there's more information out there. I've asked Shay to help me, but I'm pretty sure it'll lead nowhere, and everything will be okay. Okay? Don't worry, Ma."

"If you're sure it'll lead to nothing, then why, Richie? Why do this? Why now? Maybe..." she pursed her lips, "maybe I've been too hard on your new friend, that cop, that Rebecca. To me, she's no Isabella, but if she makes you happy, maybe I'm just gonna have to live with that."

Richie cringed at Carmela saying "she's no Isabella," but

still, it was a start. "Well, that's quite a surprise coming from you," Richie said. "And I'm glad to hear it."

"I don't know what else I can do," Carmela told him, then folded her hands together, and rolled her eyes upward in a *Madonna*-like pose. "*Figlio mio! Poverino!*" she cried, blinking hard as if to force out a tear or two.

Carmela shouting at him was bad enough, but her tears, even fake ones, were beyond his ability to handle. "What you can do, is go home and stop worrying," Richie said, standing.

Carmela's tears and wailing immediately stopped. "What's this? Go home?"

He took her arm, picked up her purse and coat, and walked her to the front door. "I'll be fine. And thank you for the manicotti."

With that, he kissed her cheek and gently shuttled her out of the house. Once he shut the door on her, he realized he'd just given his mother the bum's rush.

He sighed. He didn't know how, he didn't know when, but he knew he would pay for that, no doubt about it.

~

Rebecca and Sutter went to the San Mateo carpet warehouse where Yussef Najjar once worked. His boss there had reported him missing nine years earlier.

Chad Lompoc, the owner of the warehouse, was on the premises. "Yes, I remember Yussef," he said to the two detectives as he led them into his small, utilitarian office. "He was a good worker, and a quiet man. That was why I contacted the police when he didn't show up."

"Was there a reason you didn't go straight to his family?" Rebecca asked. Lompoc sat behind his desk, and she and Sutter faced him.

"There sure was! I didn't know he had one anywhere near. He told us that when he was a boy, he left Lebanon to come to the US to live with his uncle, but that the uncle was now dead. He never mentioned anyone else. He lived alone in a small apartment about a half mile away, close enough to walk to work. We went there, of course, and no one answered the door, or our phone calls. When the neighbors said they hadn't seen him for days, I called the police."

"Did you suspect something had happened to him?"

"Of course! We were afraid he'd been in an accident somewhere, or dead, or whatever. We were shocked when we heard he'd returned to Lebanon. He'd given no indication that he remembered much about it, and never that he was anything but happy in the US. He even talked about becoming a citizen."

Now it was Sutter's turn to ask questions. "Did Yussef have any problems with any of his fellow workers?"

"None that came to my attention."

"Was there any problem with anyone about him being from the Middle East?"

Lompoc hesitated, but then said, "A little, but whenever it came up, he said he was a Catholic. That seemed to stop the complaints—at least those that came to me. I don't know what was going on with Yussef and the others on a personal level. But I will say, everyone seemed to get along just fine."

"Did he have any close friends here?" Rebecca chimed in.

"Hmm. I'll have to look at my records. I have a lot of turnover. Delivering, unloading, and nailing down wall-to-wall carpeting is back-breaking work, and most guys only do it a few years then find something else."

The detectives waited while Lompoc called up lists of employees on his computer, and he gave them a couple of names to look into.

Sutter took the names and said he would handle them.

Rebecca was glad Sutter was willing to do that, and that her afternoon was free.

She had a plane to catch.

17

Rebecca was going to be the death of him, that was all there was to it. The day before, after dealing with Carmela, Richie had gotten a call from Vito saying that he had followed Rebecca to a BART train to the San Francisco airport. There, Vito couldn't follow her past the security gate, but she clearly had a plane ticket to somewhere. When Richie heard this, he tried phoning her. A couple of hours passed before she answered his call. He asked what she was doing, and she lied, saying she was busy in Homicide, that she'd gotten a new case and would have to work most of the night. He was ready to jump into the phone and tell her that he knew she not only was *not* in homicide, but that she probably wasn't in the whole damn state.

It took all the composure he could muster—and that wasn't much these days—to say nothing. If she wanted to be that way, so be it.

Still it rankled. What the hell was she doing? It had to be something about one of her cases, or so he guessed. Or so he hoped. The worrywart part of him wondered if it had something to do with the interesting stranger that Vito said she had had lunch with the other day. She hadn't told him about that guy either.

Vito hadn't called him back until after ten o'clock last night, when he reported Rebecca had returned home.

Richie knew he was acting ridiculously jealous, and Rebecca had never given him any cause to feel that way. It had to do with Isabella, he was sure, with the way everything about Isabella left him feeling unsettled and unsure, as if he didn't know which way was up and who he should or shouldn't trust.

He had always trusted Rebecca. He only wished she hadn't lied to him about where she was.

He should try calling her again. Ask her point blank where she was, what she was hiding. But instead of picking up the phone, he beat a hasty retreat out of his home. He couldn't bear sitting alone even one minute longer. He hated the direction his thoughts were going. He got into his car and headed to North Beach where he checked in with Don Giorgio and then went to Chinatown where he visited the Five Family Association's Milton Jang. So far, neither had found out anything about Sean Hinkle's supposed suicide. Richie had been sure that if they could tap into the rumor mill about who was behind Hinkle's death, it would be a direct line to the person who didn't like Rebecca's interference.

He also realized that, if he was smart, he would use this free time to contact Isabella's parents about her laptop. But he guessed he wasn't smart because that was the last thing he wanted to do.

Instead he concentrated on others he might know who were close to City Hall. One of his former clients came to mind—a lobbyist for the San Francisco Giants baseball team. San Francisco fans were notoriously fickle. The 49ers had moved out of the city to the Peninsula; many years ago the Warriors basketball team had moved to Oakland, and even the Giants watched their fan base shrink when the team didn't perform up to expectations.

The lobbyist, Stu Haynes, knew just about everyone in City Hall, and had worked closely with the mayor over the past few years. Richie had fixed a couple of delicate situations for Haynes over the years, one involving gambling debts, and the other involving a male prostitute. He now met Haynes at the Buena Vista near Fisherman's Wharf.

"I'm coming to you for help this time," Richie said after ordering Haynes a Macallan single malt, neat. He had arrived earlier and was nursing what look like gin-and-tonic, but without the gin.

"Uh, oh." Haynes put his hand over the wallet in his back pocket. "What's this little meeting going to cost me?"

"Nothing," Richie said. "You might have the knowledge I need." He explained about the real estate holding company and how some people in or near City Hall seemed to take an exceptional interest in it.

"Cat's already out of the bag on that one, Richie," Haynes said with a sly grin. "I already heard something about you causing some big real estate investors grief."

"Who, me?"

"Yeah, I know," Haynes smirked. "I also know our beloved mayor is doing all he can to make it easy for foreigners to buy property here."

"What do you mean by 'making it easy'?" Richie asked.

"Changing rules about certain types of property ownership. The beauty of a holding company is that the company buys the property, and the participants don't have to make their names public—especially if the holding company is headquartered in another country—like the Cayman Islands."

"So that's it," Richie said. "A way to hide wealth."

"It's one possibility," Haynes said. "But there are others. Whoever is behind crafting those new real estate rules would have a lot of power—and a lot of people indebted to him, or her. In politics, it's all about tit-for-tat."

"Who has the authority to make such rules in the city?" Richie asked.

Haynes rubbed his chin. "I suspect it would have to be the mayor or a supervisor. I don't see anyone lower being able to pull it off."

"Interesting," Richie said. Once again, he realized Rebecca's difficulties didn't stem from what she had been investigating when she looked into Audrey Poole's murder, but where it might lead.

"Our mayor is quite ambitious, you know," Haynes said. "Sacramento is most likely his next step."

"The governorship?" Richie asked.

"You got it. And I suggest you don't do anything that might put you in the way of him reaching that goal. Anyone in the way will find life has suddenly become very unhealthy."

∼

Now that Rebecca and Sutter knew something about Yussef Najjar and his family, Rebecca started the morning tracking down phone records, credit cards, bank statements, emails, and any social media accounts she could find. What emerged was a man who had a small group of male friends and an ever changing set of one- or two-time dates with women. He even spent some time on match.com, but third dates appeared to be non-existent. Rebecca couldn't tell why. He wasn't particularly handsome, but his features weren't awful. His job wasn't exciting, but at least he had one.

The only worrisome point was that his Facebook posts grew

increasingly bitter, especially about women, lambasting them for deceitfulness and lies.

Rebecca was staring at her computer when Homicide's secretary, Elizabeth Havlin, buzzed her phone. "A gentleman is here to see you. He says his name is Henry Tate."

It took a moment for the name to register: Shay. "Yes, send him in."

She should have known that Elizabeth wouldn't just "send" Shay anywhere. She led him into the Homicide bureau. Since she was trying to head toward Rebecca's desk and at the same time to stare at the handsome, well-dressed man at her side, she ended up walking right into Luis Calderon's desk.

"Hey!" Calderon shouted, then abruptly shut his mouth as Shay cast an icy glare his way.

"Sorry," Elizabeth murmured, then looked at Shay and smiled. "Right this way, Mr. Tate."

Calderon gawked, and even Rebecca could hear the slight tremolo in Elizabeth's voice. When she reached Rebecca's desk, she continued to stand there smiling at Shay.

"Thank you, Elizabeth," Rebecca said by way of dismissal, and then to Shay. "This is a surprise."

"Rebecca," he said, with a curt nod.

Elizabeth continued to gape at the two of them until Rebecca met her eye. "Oh!" she murmured, then rushed back to the front office.

Shay took the guest chair by Rebecca's desk.

"So, what brings you here?" she asked. "Did Richie send you?"

"No. I'm here on my own." Shay gave a dismissive glance at Calderon, the only detective besides Rebecca in the bureau at the moment. "I have to talk to you about your case."

"The skeleton?"

"Yes." He drew in his breath. "You've noticed I've been interested in this case. It turns out I knew the dead man."

"You knew Yussef Najjar." Her words were more a confirmation than a question.

"From the time I heard you'd found bones that had been buried for some years, I couldn't help but wonder if they belonged to Yussef. He disappeared nine years ago, and it was all very strange. Word went out that he went back to Lebanon, but I never believed that."

"Why not?"

"From things Yussef had told me. The family was split. Yussef on one side, his brother, Gebran, on the other. You've met Gebran, I imagine?"

"Yes."

"It all had to do with money and politics and old, old family feuds in the way of many Arab households—even Christian ones." He gave a slight grin, as if to say, what could be more natural than family members fighting amongst themselves? "The trouble was, a couple of the cousins didn't take anything lightly. They were serious and, I believe, deadly. I think many in the family suspected they killed Yussef. That was why no one went to the police. If they told about the cousins, it could have set off a series of deadly consequences for the family. If the cousins were accused, and the police arrested them, or even worse, if they were executed or deported and killed in Lebanon because of Yussef's murder, there would have been more killings—revenge killings."

"Did you meet these cousins?" she asked.

"No. But Yussef clearly was afraid of them."

"Why did you keep all that quiet?" she asked.

"How could I go to the police when his own family refused to? And I had no proof of anything. Frankly, I hoped he had simply left the Bay Area for some place safe."

His explanation made no sense to her. "I find it hard to believe that you, with all your knowledge of computer hacking and how to find out just about anything, didn't look more closely into what had become of your friend."

"It happened years ago. Back then, my life wasn't at all the way it is now. I had just left the military and was ... troubled, let's say." Shay paused, as if not sure how much to tell her. "It was clear to me Yussef wouldn't have wanted the family to go to war because of his death. Maybe I was wrong, but I felt it wasn't my place to interfere."

She leaned back in her chair and folded her arms. "But now you've changed your mind."

"Yes." He gave her another of his cold stares, and yet, she sensed a strangeness to his eyes—a fierce intensity not usually visible in their strange blue depths.

She felt uncomfortable looking at him, and reached for her notepad, flipping it open to a blank page. Something felt wrong about this entire story. "Do you know the names of these cousins?"

"He called them Ibrahim and Mustafa. I think their last name was also Najjar, but some of the family had the name Hariri. I'm not sure which was theirs."

"Do they live in the city?"

"They did at the time. That was the problem. Yussef took a job in San Mateo and moved there to get away from them. He kept saying he wished they'd go back to Los Angeles where they had been living and stop using his mother and wealthy brother to live off of. I don't know if they returned to LA or not."

"Can you tell me anything else about them? Age? Occupation?"

"They were around Yussef's age, so I guess they're in their late thirties or early forties now. As to occupation, no. But they weren't exactly Mensa material. That's as much as I know."

"Okay. Thanks for telling me all this." Rebecca shut the notebook. "Since you're here, I want to ask you about a very different situation. I'm wondering if you have any feel yet, as you look into Isabella's death, what might have happened to her that night?"

His eyes lost their coldness, and she actually saw concern and humanity in them. "All I can say is, I hope it was an accident. A true accident."

She understood why he said that. "Yes," she murmured. "So do I."

18

Soon after Shay left, Rebecca received a phone call from Gebran Najjar. He made it a point to tell her that he was only talking to her, a woman, because Sutter wasn't in the office.

"Fine," was her clipped, cold response.

"I called to tell you," Gebran said, "my mother passed away last night."

Rebecca was stunned...at first. His mother wasn't that old, and Rebecca's normal inclination was to suspect most anything and everything. His mother might have had dementia, but no one indicated she was close to death. It all sounded too opportune. Still, she couldn't come right out and accuse him of anything, especially something as nefarious as killing his own mother just to avoid questioning. For now, she'd take his story at face value. "I'm sorry to hear it. What happened to her?"

"She died during her sleep. I'm only glad we did not trouble her last hours on this earth with news of my brother's death."

"Yes, I'm sure that's a relief."

"Now, I hope you will allow my family to grieve, and leave

our relatives unbothered by your questions. There is nothing more we can tell you."

"We'll do what we can to respect your family in this difficult time," she said, but was now even more inclined to believe there was more to the story.

He hung up without another word.

At almost that same moment, Sutter returned to Homicide and dropped into his office chair. Before he could get comfortable, Rebecca filled him in on the conversation. "They said she had dementia, not that she was at death's door. Doesn't her passing, now, just when we want to question her, seem convenient?"

"Hard to know," Sutter said. "That family isn't exactly forthcoming. By the way, the two friends of Yussef that I found were no help. He was an okay guy. That's it. Sounded like they hardly knew him or didn't much care about him. But they gave me a few other names and phone numbers."

"And? Any luck?" she asked.

"Same thing. He was likable, but stern, quiet, and close-mouthed about anything outside work, including family and friends. Most assumed his family lived far from him, and that he only had one or two close friends, but who they were, no one could say. They also said he was bitter about women, and that women didn't seem to like him. In fact, a couple of his female coworkers admitted that he made them nervous, but they couldn't point to any specific reason why, except that he 'stared' at them a lot."

"Sounds kind of creepy," Rebecca said.

"Maybe." Sutter shrugged. End of report.

But there had to be more. They just needed to dig deeper.

"I've got an idea." With that, Rebecca phoned the Medical Examiner's office and spoke to Dr. Ramirez. She asked if the ME had been contacted about a woman named Fairuz Najjar who had died in a nursing home.

"I haven't heard a word. It's been years since I've gotten an autopsy request for a nursing home patient," Evelyn said.

"That's what I expected to hear." Rebecca thanked her and hung up.

"No dice," she said to Sutter. "Still, I'd love to request an autopsy of Fairuz. I've got questions, such as why did Fairuz die right when we were about to ask question her about Yussef's disappearance."

"Eastwood will never approve it," Sutter warned. "We have no cause."

"We need to find one," Rebecca said.

Sutter agreed. "That family, her son in particular, didn't want us to have any information. He didn't even want to tell us where his mother was living."

"Let's pay him another visit and press harder." Rebecca folded her arms, her expression unforgiving. "One way or another, I'm getting an autopsy even if I have to do it myself."

~

Before heading to the Najjar home, they needed to get all their ducks in a row, in particular, getting more background on the cousins Shay had told her about. Pouring cups of coffee for herself and Sutter, Rebecca quickly filled her partner in on her visit from Shay, giving only the briefest explanation—one that didn't mention Richie—of how she knew him. It seemed a long shot that a couple of cousins murdered Yussef, but right now, it was the only lead they had.

The two began pouring over California records for any mention of an Ibrahim and Mustafa Najjar or Hariri. Rebecca had thought the names were rare, but she soon discovered they were fairly common in California since the state housed about a third of all the Middle Eastern people in the U.S.

They found a good number of people with those names, as

well as another large group with only slight variations in the spelling.

It was a daunting task. Sutter soon began grousing that Shay's information might not be legitimate. "Just who is this guy you call Shay?" he asked at one point. "You hardly said. I hope he's not a friend of Richie's."

Rebecca ignored her partner's grumbling. He'd never warmed up to Richie, and she didn't need him going off on a tangent about Richie being involved with people with questionable reputations. Instead, she picked up the phone and contacted her source in the State Department, but Patti Flynn said it would be impossible to search all the records, especially since a lot of Arab names had a variety of spellings caused by changing from Arab script to Roman letters.

Flynn added that if the cousins left the US for Lebanon, they would be impossible to track down. A bit of news she hadn't wanted to hear.

Rebecca decided it was best not to relay any of this news to Sutter as he continued to search through names, dates of birth, and residences. She didn't want to give him an excuse to stop.

19

Richie couldn't put it off any longer.

He drove to the house on Telegraph Hill that he once thought of as a second home. Over a year had passed since he last dropped in for a quick visit, and guilt swept over him as he approached. The building, like almost all in this neighborhood, consisted of two flats. The bottom one shared ground level with the garage, and the upper flat was larger, taking up the entire floor.

After ringing the doorbell, he heard a buzz and pushed open the door. "Hello," he called as he climbed the long staircase to the top floor.

"Richie! Can it be?" Dolores Russo had come down a few steps and leaned over the banister to see who had walked in. "It's so good to see you."

He all but ran up the rest of the stairs to greet her with a kiss on the cheek and a long hug. She hugged him back, then studied his face. "You're looking good, Richie. A little too thin, but that's because you don't come here anymore to eat my ravioli."

He grinned. "I will, Dolores, I promise."

"I know, I know." The way she said it, she knew he wouldn't be going there to eat. Some things were impossible to go back to. "Come have some vino with me. I have some *braciole* left over from last night. A little bite, okay?"

"Sure. That sounds great."

He sat at the kitchen table while she poured him some Italian red and heated the *braciole*, thinly sliced beef smeared with minced garlic and parsley, then rolled up and cooked in a red sauce until the meat could be cut with a fork. With it, she put out sourdough bread. Between the aroma of her cooking, the taste of the food, and sitting in her kitchen, memories flooded him. He didn't know if he wanted to smile from how great those memories were, or cry because, while they would always be part of his past, no new ones would be made again in this house.

"It's good to see you, Dolores," he said softly.

"Yes, for me, too," she murmured. Her voice was husky, and she gave a little cough to hide it, then reached for her wine. She squeezed his hand, and he knew she was having similar thoughts.

They both finished the wine a little too quickly, and she poured second glasses. Before long, they were talking the way they used to. She was filled with curiosity about Big Caesar's, and Richie regaled her with stories of crazy musicians, singers, and customers he had to deal with. One thing about Richie, he always had stories that could make people laugh. Some people told him it was a gift. If so, right now, he was glad he had it.

When the food and wine were gone, he said, "I actually had a reason for stopping by—a reason besides wanting to see you again."

"I'm not surprised," she admitted. "So, what is it?"

"I recently heard that the police gave you a laptop that Isabella had with her on the night.... Anyway, I was wondering if you still have it."

"A laptop?" she said. "Oh, from the police, you said. I probably still have it. The stuff they gave us, I didn't even want to look at it. I had Ray put everything in the basement. Let's go down there. I'll find it for you. But why do you want to see it?"

"It's probably nothing," he said. "I'm just curious. You know me."

She gave him a strange look. "Yes, I do know you. Okay, you won't say. That's all right. I don't think I really want to know. *Andiamo.*"

In the basement of the building, Dolores found the box the police had given her and her husband. She stepped outside as Richie opened it. He realized someone, probably Isabella's father, Ray, had gone through it to remove Isabella's wallet and her jewelry, including her engagement ring. He had insisted that the diamond ring be buried with her. Bloodied clothes, her handbag, shoes, and a laptop were still in the box.

He took out the laptop, and then shut the box once more, folding its flaps back down. He felt his entire body shake as he did it—almost as if he were burying her again.

Then he took a deep breath. With the laptop under his arm, he said goodbye to Dolores and left the house as quickly as he could.

20

Rebecca and Sutter returned to the Najjar home that evening to see Gebran.

Rebecca would have preferred not to let anyone in the family know that she was trying to find the two cousins Shay had told her about, but since she was having no luck whatsoever locating them, she had no choice but to ask for help.

And then there was the issue of an autopsy.

After long moments of knocking, Salma opened the door, and frowned. "We are in mourning," she said softly.

"We understand," Rebecca said. "But we have questions."

Salma led them up the stairs to the living room. The boy was playing a video game on the TV, and the daughter was nowhere to be seen. Gebran sent the boy to his room.

Rebecca and Sutter gave their condolences to Gebran over his mother's death and refused any of the tea Salma offered. Rebecca quickly got to the point. "We were putting together some information about the case, and we need to talk about two of your cousins, Mr. Najjar. I'm hoping you can give me information about where to find them."

"Cousins? What cousins?" Gebran's tone was harsh.

"Ibrahim and Mustafa. I'm told their last names are Najjar or Hariri," Rebecca said.

Gebran looked confused. "I have no cousins with those names. Not in this country, anyway. My mother's younger brother is named Ibrahim Bassil, but he lives in France. I have never seen him."

Rebecca remembered what the State Department analyst said about Arab names. Maybe Shay wasn't given the right ones. "I heard that there were a number of disagreements between you, Yussef, and these cousins."

"No." His voice was loud now. "I have no such cousins."

"Would you tell me the names of any cousins who live nearby?"

Gebran glared at Salma and spoke low and quickly in Arabic, gesturing toward Rebecca and Sutter.

Salma sat up straighter and spoke. "My mother-in-law had a brother who lived in this country. He sent for Fairuz to come here when she was widowed many years ago. He and his wife—they're both deceased—had only one child, a daughter. She now lives in Los Angeles. She has three children, but we've only met them once when we brought our children to Disneyland. She is the only cousin my husband knows in this country."

"What about cousins from his father's side?"

"They would still be in Lebanon. His father's family never liked Fairuz. After his father died, those relatives ignored Fairuz and her two sons. That was why she was happy to leave Lebanon and come here to be with her brother."

"I see." Rebecca thought a moment, and remembered how Richie, at his cousin Angie's wedding, had introduced her to several older women he called "Zia" and they weren't really his aunts. "Were there any close friends Yussef might have called cousins, even if they weren't related?"

"No," Gebran said firmly. "How many times must I tell you?"

"Do you know anyone named Ibrahim or Mustafa who are

not cousins?" Rebecca asked finally, growing increasingly frustrated.

"Do you have any idea how common those names are in my community?" Gebran asked. "If so, you wouldn't insult me with such a stupid question!"

Rebecca gave him a hard look, then faced Salma. "Mrs. Najjar, what about you? Have you heard those names before?"

"Not in connection with Yussef, or as friends of this family. I mean, there are many people with those names, as my husband said, but no one stands out." At that, she dropped her gaze to the floor.

Gebran gruffly stated, "No friends here, and no cousins. No real cousins; no fake cousins." He folded his arms and glared at the detectives.

"Well," Sutter said as he and Rebecca stood, "we didn't mean to intrude. Just one last question before we go. Which nursing home was your mother in?"

"Why do you want to know?" Gebran growled.

"Just to make sure we have all necessary information. That question was left unanswered last time we were here."

Gebran's jaw tightened. His eyes narrowed, but at long last he spat out, "Pacific House."

"Thank you. And what is the doctor showing as her cause of death, Mr. Najjar?"

"As I told your partner, she had a heart attack."

Sutter glanced at Rebecca then back at Gebran. "I assume an autopsy is being performed?"

"Of course not! She will not be defiled. Her doctor knows —*knew*—her condition well. He stated she had a heart attack."

"Where is your mother's body now?" Rebecca asked. Gebran gave the name of a mortuary reluctantly, angrily.

Now, with their interview of Gebran ended, Rebecca and Sutter were about to leave when Rebecca faced Gebran with one last question. "When did you last see your mother?"

Gebran stiffened. "I visited her last night."

Two detectives eyed each other and nodded. "Thank you for your time," Sutter said, as they left the house.

As soon as Rebecca and Sutter got back to their cars, she called Lt. Eastwood to see if he was willing to authorize an autopsy. He still believed they didn't have a sufficient cause, but he was willing to holding the body as they continued the investigation.

Rebecca then called the mortuary and told them the Homicide Division of the San Francisco Police Department was now interested in Fairuz Najjar's death, and that they were not to touch the body until given the okay to do so. Somehow, she was going to get that autopsy.

∽

Richie could scarcely believe it when he saw Rebecca standing in his doorway. He'd been alone, moping and miserable since returning home from the visit to Dolores Russo.

"I was hoping you hadn't left yet for Big Caesar's," she said with a smile.

It felt good to see Rebecca's smiling face. "I've been debating if I want to go at all tonight. Come on in."

"I wondered how you're doing," she said, removing her leather jacket as she walked into the living room. "It's been a couple of days."

"I know. I've been trying not to think about much. Go to work, keep my head down," he said. *Go visit sad, old friends.* He felt strangely awkward having her there. "Sometimes, so much happens it gets a bit overwhelming."

"I agree."

He sought her gaze, and as he held it, words quickly spilled from his lips. "I'm glad you're here."

"So am I" she told him.

He gestured toward the kitchen. "Would you like something to drink? Wine? Beer? Coffee?"

"Coffee sounds good, especially since I brought a couple of apple fritters." She held up a small white bakery bag. "I know how much you love them."

In the kitchen, she tore open the bag and put it on the table. Then she opened the back door and stepped out onto the deck while he used his espresso machine to make them each an Americano.

As the coffeemaker whirred, he joined her. The air was crisp, the night surprisingly warm. Behind her, the fog had lifted and the full moon was clearly visible. Rebecca by moonlight; he could stare at her that way for hours, he realized.

Right after leaving Isabella's home, he had thought about going to see Rebecca. But what should he say? That going to his former fiancée's home had made him sad and upset? That seemed wrong. It wasn't her problem, after all. So, instead, he came home.

Now, he realized that keeping away from her hadn't helped at all. In fact, the more he stayed away, the more angry he felt at himself. He was torn between some vague notion of "disloyalty" to Isabella and wanting to see the one person who made him feel alive.

He brushed a quick kiss across her lips, tamping back his desire for more, much more. This wasn't the time. "Coffee's ready," he said, taking her hand and walking back inside.

They sat at the kitchen table with their coffee, and each took a big bite of fritter. "Delicious," Richie said. "How did you know I was hungry?"

"When aren't you hungry?" she said with a smile. "I was, too, but I didn't want to stop for dinner and miss seeing you."

"I'm glad you stopped by, fritters or no fritters."

Their conversation felt stilted, not at all what he wanted, but Isabella's death kept coming between them. He wanted their relationship to get back where it had been, but it couldn't, not until he had answers.

Rebecca picked the last remaining crumb of the fritter from the plate and popped it in her mouth. Resting her arms on the table, she looked straight at Richie and asked softly, "Have you picked up the laptop yet?"

He nodded. "I dropped it off at Shay's. He'll figure it out."

She continued to watch him, as if trying to read his mind. "Are you okay?"

"No."

The word seemed to upset her. "No?" she whispered.

"No. That fritter told me how hungry I am." He tried hard to sound upbeat. "Let's go get something to eat."

"No," she said flatly.

Had he heard right? "No? Why not?"

"I'd rather stay right here with you." Her large blue eyes captured his, and wouldn't let go. "We need to talk. Just you and me. Here. Where it's quiet and we won't be disturbed."

"All right," he said, but picked up his cell phone. "I'll order takeout and have it delivered. How about Indonesian?"

"Sounds good." He ordered the food, and the two went into the living room where he put Rachmaninoff's Second Symphony on the stereo, and then joined her on the sofa.

"Do you want to talk about it?" she asked.

He knew she was referring to his visit to Isabella's parents. "No. Not at all. Or, at least, not yet."

She nodded, but he knew she wouldn't give up. Eventually they'd have to talk about it. "Then why don't we talk about Shay?"

"Shay?" That got his attention.

"I'm concerned about him," she said. "I can't prove it, but I believe he sent me on a wild goose chase." She told him about Shay's visit to Homicide, and that the Najjar family denied having any cousins or even knowing anyone with the names he had given her. Also, when she and Sutter scoured California records for anyone with those names, the people they found didn't meet the profile Shay had given her of the cousins.

As Richie took in the story, he had to admit that something seemed a bit off about Shay these days. But Shay was so reserved and close mouthed, he had hesitated to ask. "It makes no sense," he said. "Why would Shay do such a thing?"

"Has Shay ever spoken to you about any of those people? Or any Lebanese or Arab friends?"

"Not at all, although I didn't know him nine years ago. We only met some six years back through Vito."

"Vito? That surprises me," she said. "Those two couldn't be more different."

"That's for damn sure," he said with a small smile. "But Vito has a cousin who was in the Special Forces and was having some PTSD issues. He'd been a sniper. Someone had the vet talk to Shay, and that was how he and Vito met. Vito was floored by the guy—by his skills, his background, and his knowledge."

"Shay was a sniper?" Rebecca asked. "That explains a lot."

Richie nodded. "With the Marines. I know Shay doesn't look or act like anyone who could talk to a vet about PTSD, but apparently, he was a big help. Normally, he doesn't talk to anyone about his past. And that includes me. I know he had been really good with computers from a young age and got a degree in computer sciences when he was only twenty. He started working in Silicon Valley, but apparently hated it there. He quit and joined the Marines. Talk about a career change. But that, too, wasn't right. He didn't re-up and at twenty-five he found himself in San Francisco. Here, he saw that if he pulled his tech knowledge together with learning more about businesses, he could do all right for himself. Somehow, he managed to get himself an MBA from the Wharton School of Business. And then, he really started pulling in money. That was when I met him. It seemed he had the Midas touch. Anything he touched turned a profit, and he didn't let rules and regulations get in his way."

"I've never heard of a résumé like that," Rebecca said.

"I know, but then, how many people are like Shay? Actually, it was Vito who filled in a lot of the blanks for me. According to Vito, Shay put what he learned in Afghanistan together with his computer knowledge, business, and finance, and ended up working for people who were willing to pay him unheard of amounts of money. Most were less-than-admirable, but in time, he was rich enough to work for whoever he wanted, and to cut out the sleaze. Whether any of Vito's account is true, I have no idea. But I do know that Shay's biggest problem is boredom. He claims that's why he likes getting my calls. My cases are anything but boring."

"No kidding," she said, grinning. "But that still doesn't explain why he lied to me about the Najjar family."

"You aren't sure he lied."

"Well, somebody's lying. I don't trust Gebran, and his wife seems to go along with whatever he wants, but I can't find any hint of the cousins Shay mentioned."

"I'll talk to him," Richie said.

"No, don't. I don't want him to think I'm complaining to you," Rebecca said. "But why would he tell me something like that if it wasn't true?"

Richie shook his head. He hadn't any idea, but Rebecca's assumption, as absurd as it sounded, made him want to know the truth, and if Rebecca couldn't get it, he would.

"I wonder if the Najjar family remembers Shay," she said. "Do you have a picture of him I can borrow?"

"He doesn't like having his picture taken," Richie said.

"So I've noticed." Then, she flashed an all-knowing smile. "But you do a lot of things people don't like."

"I can probably find what you need," he said, then grinned.

She didn't grin or laugh in return. Instead, she reached out and caressed his cheek. "I need more than that."

So did he.

He wove his fingers through her hair, drawing her ever closer. Being with Rebecca, talking with her, simply sitting close took his mind off so much that haunted him. He needed her. All of her.

Now.

He kissed her softly. But quickly, the kiss deepened. He was losing himself...

All too suddenly she tore away. "Richie," she said breathlessly. "I think I heard the doorbell ring."

It took a moment for her words to register. The bell rang again and reality set in. "Oh, hell."

Dinner had arrived.

Talk about lousy timing.

21

The next afternoon, Shay stopped by Richie's home. "That laptop was a treasure trove," he said. "Everything we need. I'd like to hold on to it for a while, if that's okay."

"Of course," Richie said. The two men sat in the living room. Shay had a cup of tea, and Richie poured himself some coffee, anxious to hear what Shay had learned, even though he hated the thought of learning that Isabella's death was more than tragic—but was murder, the details of which were becoming clearer all the time. Still, he was glad he could finally think about and talk about Isabella without needing strong liquor at his side.

"It was the bank's laptop," Shay continued. "I'm surprised they hadn't demanded it back, except that whoever was behind the holding company scheme probably feared asking for it would put more attention on it than it had gotten to that point. And that would have been bad."

"Really?" Richie asked.

"Isabella not only figured out what was going on between API Holding and the bank, she had proof it was illegal. What she planned to do about it was anyone's guess."

"Even if she had that information, where would she be going that early with it?"

"That's what I'm working on. The four people we already identified are the same ones I'm seeing in Isabella's material. Three live in Marin County, where we assume she was headed: Skarzer, Yamada, and Egerton. Ethan Nolan, the data operations manager, has only lived in the city. I'm thinking Isabella was either going to Marin to confront the person behind the scheme, or to tell someone about it."

Richie shook his head. "Amazing. See what more you can find out about those four, and I'll also do a little personal digging. You know the routine."

"Will do. Anything else you'd like me to look into?" Shay asked.

"No, but I would like you to answer a question," Richie said.

"Oh?"

"Rebecca told me not to say anything, but she suspects you sent her on some wild goose chase, looking for cousins of a dead man—cousins who don't exist." Richie stopped talking, waiting for a denial or explanation.

"She does? Why? Because she can't find them?" Shay's voice was as cold as Richie had ever heard it.

"What's going on?" Richie asked. "You're not yourself. Even Rebecca knows it. She's looking for a killer, and you've been curious about the victim since I first mentioned that someone found a skeleton out in Golden Gate Park."

"It sounds like she's becoming as paranoid as you are," Shay said with a smirk. "You're having a bad influence on her."

"Funny guy. Look, I don't want to be caught between the two of you," Richie said. "But if you do anything that hurts Rebecca or her investigation, you'll answer to me."

"I'm not trying to hurt her." Shay rose to his feet and his eyes were sadder than Richie had ever seen them. "I'm trying to help someone else."

Rebecca drove to the Pacific House nursing home. It was a place with mostly Medi-Cal patients, California's version of welfare with medical costs. Rebecca went to the front office, showed her badge, and asked to speak to the head of the facility.

She didn't have to wait long. An older woman with frizzy gray hair held off her face by a couple of bobby pins on each side stepped out of an office. "I'm Ruth Willis, Pacific House's director," she said. "May I help you?"

"Yes." Rebecca introduced herself. "I'd like to speak to you about one of your former patients, Fairuz Najjar."

"Surely. But you're in homicide? Why—?"

"Just routine, for now," Rebecca said.

Willis looked surprisingly nervous. "Oh, I see. Well, poor woman just passed a couple of days ago. Please come into my office."

Rebecca entered the spartan office and took a seat. "I understand Mrs. Najjar was suffering from dementia, and that her death may have been unexpected."

"It's hard to say. Yes, she had developed heart issues, and the end came more quickly than expected, that is true. But that doesn't usually involve homicide, or any police—"

"What happened to her?" Rebecca interrupted.

Willis swallowed hard. "She was fine at nine o'clock when it was time for lights out, but when we did bed checks at midnight, we found her dead."

"Did someone see her at nine?"

"Yes. We go into each room, shut off the overhead light, make sure the person is comfortable, has water by their bed, and so on."

"You're sure she had no complaints at nine o'clock?"

Willis turned to her computer screen. "We're quite up-to-date here. We log-in every interaction with our guests."

"Guests?" Rebecca asked.

"Patients, in your parlance," Willis explained. She then studied the screen. "Najjar ... where is she? Ah, here we go."

She turned the monitor so that Rebecca could also see it. "Here," she said. "You can see we've logged-in our bed checks, what she ate for breakfast, lunch, dinner. She had a visitor at seven that evening, and we had to ask the visitor to leave at nine when the facility shuts down for the night."

"Who was the visitor?"

"That would be on our sign-in sheet." Willis phoned for the sheets to be brought to her.

"But Fairuz was fine when the last visitor left?" Rebecca asked. "Did much time pass between the visit and the staff's bed check?"

"The staffer is here now. I'll call her in." Willis used an intercom to request that "Abby" report to Mrs. Willis's office. At the same time, the receptionist brought in the sign-in sheets and handed them to Willis.

"Okay, let's see." She ran her finger along the sheet. "Here we go. Gebran, the son, dropped in after work for about ten minutes. And later, Salma Najjar, that's the daughter-in-law, arrived at eight and signed out at nine-oh-five."

Just then, there was a knock on the door, and a young woman stuck her head in.

"Abby, come in. This is Inspector Mayfield. From Homicide. She's asking about Fairuz Najjar." Willis paused as Rebecca and the young woman greeted each other and then continued. "When you looked in on Mrs. Najjar for the nine o'clock bed check, how did she look to you?"

Abby's face turned red, and her expression stricken as her eyes jumped from her boss to the policewoman watching her.

Finally, she gazed at the ceiling as she spoke. "She seemed okay, I think. Her daughter-in-law was with her, and she said she'd take care of getting her water and shutting off the lights. I didn't want to throw her out of the room so I could do those things, so I said okay. I thought that was the nicer thing to do—to let the family help, and all. I hope that was all right."

Willis gaped at Abby a long moment. "I see," she murmured. "Thank you. We'll talk later." She regained some poise and said to Rebecca, "It's our belief that our patients like to be with family members as long as possible. We encourage the little things—such as family saying goodnight..."

Abby nodded and turned to leave when Rebecca said, "Wait. You're saying you didn't actually see Mrs. Najjar at nine o'clock?"

Abby glanced from Willis to Rebecca, and then stared at the floor. "I did see her. She was in bed."

"But," Rebecca continued, "you didn't go back to check on her after Salma Najjar left the room?"

"I had to do my rounds," Abby explained. "We only have so much time—"

"But you checked on her at midnight?"

"No. My shift ended at ten. The night shift handles midnight bed checks."

"Was it common for Salma Najjar to stay here that late at night?" Rebecca asked.

Abby scrunched her face. "No. I'm not sure she's ever done it. Not alone, at any rate. When Mrs. Najjar first came here, her son would come by a lot, and Salma was often with him. But that was pretty much it."

"Okay, Abby," Rebecca said. "You've been a big help. Thank you."

Abby finally smiled, then looked cautiously at Willis.

"Go," Willis said. And Abby did.

Rebecca turned to Willis. "Thank you for your help." She was about to leave when she asked, "Do you by any chance, have a back door I could use to leave?"

"A back door? Certainly, I'll show you where it is. Is anything wrong?"

"No, not really. I just want to surprise someone."

Before Rebecca left the office, however, she phoned Lt. Eastwood and gave him all the information she had amassed. Finally Eastwood agreed an autopsy was in order. Rebecca contacted the mortuary and the ME's office with instructions. Then, she left the nursing home.

~

Rebecca peered around the side of the building to the parking lot in front of the nursing home. As she suspected, there was Vito sitting in a car she didn't recognize and watching the home's front door.

She crept up to the car and tapped on the passenger side window.

Vito nearly jumped out of his seat. He spun toward her, his hand hovering over the jacket pocket where she suspected he kept his firearm while driving. When he saw Rebecca glowering at him, his mouth dropped open. "Wha--"

She pulled open the door and got inside. "I've seen you following me for a few days now," she said. "I know Richie's been worried about me, but really, isn't this a bit ridiculous? I understand the danger now. I'm convinced, okay? I can take care of myself."

Vito swallowed hard. "The boss says that you're in danger, so I gotta do this."

She sneered. "I don't think so."

"Look Inspector, I only do what I'm told," he said.

"Good, then I'm telling you to knock it off."

She started to get back out of the car when he suddenly added, "If you want the truth, it *does* look to me like you're pretty safe. But, also, if you want the truth, it's the boss I'm worried about. Somebody's following him, that's for sure."

She eased back onto the passenger seat, alarm bells going off in her head. She stared at Vito. "Somebody's following Richie? Really?"

"I wouldn't kid about that. Not to you, anyway. All I know is, it's too bad I can't be two places at once—sort of like that Italian saint my mother likes to talk about, Padre Pio. During World War II in Italy, there were a lot of stories about how he used to be seen in two places at one time. No lie. But, I guess this ain't really like no war, is it?"

"It's going to become a war," Rebecca said, "if Richie keeps on having you follow me when he's the one in danger. Who's behind this? Do you know?"

"I'm not sure." Vito looked worried, as if he wanted to say something but didn't know if he should or not. Finally, he dropped his gaze.

"Does this have anything to do with Isabella?" Rebecca asked softly.

He gawked at her. "You know?"

"Yes, I do. I've even been looking into her situation myself, a little at least. And the damned part of it is, Richie might be right. There were definitely some strange things going on at that bank. But what's important right now is that I don't need you following me, I don't want you following me, and I will not *have* you following me any longer. Watch Richie!"

"But what if—"

"If nothing! This whole thing—he's too emotional about it. That puts him in danger. You've got to be there for him, Vito. I need you to be."

Vito looked at her sadly. "I think you're right."

She smiled, then leaned over and gave him a quick kiss on his jowly cheek. "Thank you."

With that, she got out of the car, only glancing back to see that Vito had blushed fifty shades of red.

22

That same afternoon, Shay sat alone in his living room. It was all he could do not to jump into his car, drive to Salma's home and demand answers. How could she keep his daughter a secret? He was sure the girl was his. Her age was right, and her features were so much like those of his family—what little he remembered of it—especially the blue of her eyes. It was scary.

He could be wrong, but he had a hard time imagining Gebran Najjar fathering a girl like the one he saw. And yet, if she were his child ... His mind went round and round with the thought of it, the crazy, irrational thought of it.

It made him wonder if Gebran ever had doubts, given everything else that had happened back then.

How ironic it was that, all those years ago, Salma had worried about trusting Shay, and thought him overly tough and fearsome. She even used to say she was a little afraid of him. He scoffed at the memory. He had been scarcely more than a tiger cub in those days. A little scary, perhaps a little dangerous. But nothing like today. Back then, he hadn't yet learned how to use his experiences and training to be sure no one ever got the better of him. And he hadn't yet taught himself how to shut down all his feelings so that he no longer cared about anyone or anything, including himself.

The 'not caring' was what truly made a man frightening.

Now, she would be right not to trust him.

Memories filled him of when he first met her and how trusting she had been of strangers, of people in general. In those days, she left the curtains of her home open wide for anyone to see what was going on inside. Burglars, robbers, rapists, or simply harmless peeping Toms could look in with impunity. She hadn't thought about them. He had warned her; had explained about the world. Maybe too much; maybe too harshly.

But at least she had listened to his words of caution.

The irony of it was, if she had been wary of strangers, she never would have talked to him that day down at Aquatic Park, a small beach area along the north bay. It had a long pier from which people liked to fish. A baby seal had become caught in a fishing line. It had turned and twisted so much the line had become tangled around it, causing it to nearly drown. People were watching, but no one acted.

He waded into the water and caught the line, dragged the seal close and then held its mouth shut so it wouldn't bite as he cut the line from its flippers. Once freed, he let it go.

Others cheered and walked away as soon as the seal swam off, but she stayed to make sure Shay was all right, that he hadn't been bitten or scratched, or suffered in any other way.

She had her son with her, a boy of three named Adam. She had brought him to the beach to play in the sand. She said it was far from her house, and that she liked being far away sometimes. He found that to be an odd statement

He was only twenty-five at the time, and she was twenty-eight. He had recently returned from Afghanistan and was out of the Marines, out of work, and bitter and troubled by much of what he had seen and faced and done. He had learned to doubt that any innocence was left in the world. And then he met Salma.

That first day, they sat on the sand and talked until his trouser legs, shoes and socks dried. And still they sat and talked.

He asked if she would be coming to Aquatic Park again, and she said yes. Next week, same time, same day.

He was there. And again the week following, and for weeks thereafter.

As he sat now, remembering, he realized he couldn't leave things as they were. He had to see her—to warn her, let her know how far Rebecca's investigation had progressed, and to talk to her about their daughter. He knew, if he hurried, he would have a couple of hours before Gebran returned home.

∽

Rebecca rang the doorbell at the Najjar home. She had decided it was time, probably past time, for her to speak to Salma without Gebran hovering over her like some ghoul.

Salma answered the door. She was looking gaunt, dressed in jeans, an old tee-shirt, and unwashed hair pulled back in a barrette.

"Is your husband here?" Rebecca asked.

"No. When he was told his mother's body would undergo an autopsy, he became very angry. I believe he may be complaining to people at police headquarters at this very time."

Rebecca nodded. It was hardly unexpected news.

"I have some questions for you," Rebecca said.

Salma nodded. "Come in. My children are at school. I was just doing some cleaning."

They sat in the living room. Rebecca accepted the tea

offered, black tea made with cardamom, honey and lemon. "This tea is delicious," Rebecca said. "I like the spices in it."

"It's a popular way to serve tea in Lebanon," Salma said. "My husband enjoys it."

"How long have you been married?"

"Fourteen years. I was living in Beirut with my father—my mother died when I was very young. Since we are Christian, and many different political and religious groups fight there, my father was afraid for our safety and wanted to leave the country. He heard from one of Fairuz's relatives that Gebran was looking for a Maronite wife from the old country. Since I knew English and had gone to school, he contacted Fairuz and told her about me. Gebran brought us both to this country. He gave my father a job at his dry cleaners, and I married him."

"How old were you?"

"I was twenty-three. My father was afraid I was already an old maid."

"How did you feel about marrying like that?" Rebecca asked.

Salma stared at the floor a moment, then raised her eyes, her jaw firm. "I didn't think anything of it. It's common in my country to have the family plan a marriage, and this helped my father get away from a place he had come to fear, and to get him a job. Gebran is a good and generous man."

"I see." Rebecca turned to a different line of questioning. "I was told that some men argued with Yussef right before he disappeared. Although your husband indicated he knew of no such men, I wonder if you have any idea who they might be."

"No, I don't," she said.

"Do you know of anyone who might have fought with Yussef?"

"I'm sorry, but no."

Rebecca almost hated to take the next step, but she was stymied. From her handbag, she took the picture of Shay that

Richie had taken with his phone one night at Big Caesar's when Shay was doing some surveillance work for him. Richie had printed it for her.

"I want you to look at a photograph." Rebecca placed the photo on the table, then pointed at Shay. "Do you know this man?"

Salma paled as she stared hard at the photo. She said nothing.

"You know him, don't you?" Rebecca said.

"I don't think so." She scarcely whispered, but kept her gaze fixed on the photo.

"Don't you? He's connected with this family. I don't know how, yet, but I'll find out. We have many ways of finding out," she emphasized.

Salma turned her head away.

Rebecca watched her carefully. "You *do* remember him. I see it in your face."

Salma shook her head. "I'm not sure."

"Do you expect him to keep quiet about what happened to Yussef? He was Yussef's friend or so I've heard."

"His friend?" Questioning eyes met Rebecca's. The idea of the two men as friends seemed to puzzle her, and Rebecca wondered if Shay had lied about that, too.

"Tell me what's going on, Salma," Rebecca all but pleaded. "What does this man have to do with your family?"

"Please," Salma whispered, increasingly agitated. "Don't do this."

"I'll do whatever it takes."

"I can't ... I don't know anything!"

"We're going to Homicide." Rebecca stood, her voice cold. "Maybe there your memory will return."

"My children are in school. I need to pick them up when class ends."

"You can call someone to pick them up for you. Or call the school to keep them until you're able to get them."

She shook her head, then squared her shoulders. "My husband will be very upset if he hears you are questioning me. Please, I need to get my children myself."

Rebecca was surprised by this answer. "I'm afraid you don't have a choice unless your memory improves substantially and quickly."

Salma's lips tightened, then she nodded. "Fine. As you wish." With that, she began gathering up some papers and keys, and stuffed them into a large tote. "I'll go call the school."

She put the bag on her shoulder, and then stepped into the kitchen to make the call. Rebecca listened as she did. When the call ended, she waited for Rebecca at the top of the stairs. "Go ahead. I'll lock up behind you," she said.

Rebecca had taken a couple of steps on the stairs when she caught a glimpse of movement from the corner of her eye. She turned around just as Salma swung the tote at her. Something heavy hit the side of her head, and then all went black.

∼

Shay saw Rebecca's SUV parked outside Salma's house. Too late for a warning, he thought. He was pondering if he should stay or go when Salma's garage door opened. He parked the Maserati just as Salma backed out. She was alone.

As she pulled onto the street, he got out of his car and stood in front of her.

She slammed on the brakes and stared at him as if he were a ghost.

He went to the driver's door, but it was locked. "Roll down the window."

She hesitated a moment, then did as he asked. "Shay, my God. How..."

"I know what's going on," he said, gripping the window frame. "Where's Rebecca?"

Her large brown eyes searched his face as if trying to delve into his very soul, but then she dropped her gaze. "I pushed her down the stairs. She ... she's not moving. But she wanted to arrest me!"

His heart sank. "God, Salma! Go to my house." He gave her the address. "I'll be right there, but I've got to see to Rebecca."

"Wait." She placed her hand atop his. "Your skin is warm. You're real. I thought so many times ... But how can you be here now? Why?"

"Wait for me. I'll be there soon." He went into the garage and then to the door that led to the home's interior. There, he stopped and looked her way.

Her gaze was piercing, as if she still couldn't believe it was really him, then she pushed the remote to shut the garage door as she drove off.

Shay used the interior door from the garage to reach Rebecca. Relief filled him as he saw that she was attempting to sit up, but looked dazed. He helped her to sit and lean back against the wall, and then he knelt by her side. "Are you all right?"

"Shay? What are you—?"

"Can you stand? Let's get you to a hospital."

He helped her to her feet. She was woozy. "She—Salma—must have put something heavy in her bag and hit me as I was on the stairs. I never should have trusted her." She gazed up at Shay. "Where is she? And what are you doing here? How did you get inside the house?"

"We'll talk later." He held her arm, his other hand against her waist. "Does anything feel broken?"

"No. I don't think so."

He continued to hold her. "I'm taking you to a hospital."

"No. I just need to sit awhile. I'll be okay."

He led her from the house to his car. "In that case, I'm taking you to Richie's. You need watching. You've probably got a concussion."

"I need to go to work. I've got to find her."

"You will. I doubt she has many places to go. But first, we need to take care of you."

"If you can help me get home..."

"Richie's house is closer, and when I tell him what happened, he'll want to see you. I think you'll be better off at his place."

Shay phoned Richie as he drove, and Richie was waiting at the top of the stairs as Shay turned into his driveway. He ran down and helped Rebecca from the Maserati.

Shay watched the two slowly walk up the stairs to the front door, Richie's arm tightly around Rebecca's waist for support. Before they turned around or thought of asking him any questions such as why was he outside the Najjar home, he sped away.

23

Richie helped Rebecca to the bed in his guest room. She took off her jacket as he pulled back the covers, put a bunch of pillows on the bed, and then had her sit as he helped her remove her boots and jeans. She stretched out on the bed, and he covered her with blankets. "You doing okay?" he asked.

"I really don't need to be fussed over."

"From what Shay told me, you must have been out cold for a while. You need to take it easy. If I see signs that I don't like, you're going to the hospital whether you want to or not."

She touched the side of her head. "I don't know what that woman found in the kitchen to put in her tote bag, but it was heavy. I've got quite a lump."

"An iron? Maybe a cast-iron fry pan? Who knows? Whatever, thank God you've got such a hard head. And that you weren't hurt falling down the stairs." He gently ran his hands over her arms and held her hands. "You weren't, were you?"

"Just some bruises, thank goodness."

He kissed her forehead. "What can I get you?"

"How about some water? And an ice pack."

He soon stepped back into the bedroom with her glass of

water and a thin towel wrapped around crushed ice. Sitting on the edge of the bed, he rested the ice pack gingerly against the lump on her head, and listened as she phoned Sutter to tell him about her conversation with Salma Najjar and how the woman had managed to get away. He noted that she didn't mention Shay at all, but told him she'd called Richie for help—she might have a concussion and that was why she wasn't thinking straight and hadn't followed protocol. It sounded as if Sutter was reassuring her, saying he would tell Eastwood what had happened, then head over to the Najjar home, talk to Gebran, and try to locate Salma.

"Take backup," Rebecca said. "It's possible Salma did this to warn Gebran. He might be our killer." She and Sutter spoke a bit more, then Rebecca ended the call.

Richie sat on the edge of the bed. "What's all this about?" he asked, handing her the glass so she could take a sip of water. "And why is Shay involved?"

She took a quick drink and attempted to relax in the pillows in spite of pain that seemed to radiate from every part of her body. She then told him what little she knew. "I'm not sure how deeply Shay's involvement goes."

"I'll see what I can find out," Richie told her.

"Are you going out now?"

"And miss the chance to stay here with you and play doctor?" He mischievously waggled his eyebrows.

"Ooh, don't make me laugh, Doc. It hurts my ribs."

He kissed her gently on the lips. "I know. Believe me, having you here all night, in bed and untouchable, is going to hurt me a lot more than it does you."

∼

When Shay returned to his apartment, no one but Mrs. Brannigan was there. "Did a woman come by here this evening?" he asked.

"A woman?" Mrs. Brannigan said. "If one had, you'd have found me stretched out on the floor in shock. And then mortified because the dinner I prepared for you tonight is only enough for one. So, no. It's been just me here, same as always."

"Thanks, I guess." Sometimes he didn't know why he put up with her.

"Your supper will be on the table in ten minutes, Mr. Tate."

He was about to tell her he wasn't hungry, but realized that would cause her even more surprise and consternation than his simple question about a visitor had.

As soon as she returned to the kitchen, he went to the living room window and searched the street for Salma's blue Honda Civic. It wasn't there. He wondered if she would come over as he had asked, or if she would simply keep going. But where would she go? And why? She should go to the police, tell them everything. She, at least, would be safe then. But somehow, he knew she wouldn't.

He ate the dinner of shepherd's pie that Mrs. Brannigan had made him. Despite what Richie and others thought, he actually enjoyed well-seasoned hearty meals. He just didn't like eating food prepared by strangers. He'd seen too many truly horrible kitchens and filthy cooks in his travels to want to contemplate what he might be served in a public restaurant. He knew it was an idiosyncrasy, but that was better than having his gag reflex take over as old scenes played in his head. Or even worse, scenes of friends being shot as they sat in some supposedly safe public place and ate.

He put the dirty dishes in the sink, and made himself a Scotch and soda, then returned to the living room. The sun was setting, casting a reddish glow in the room. He took a seat and waited.

Mrs. Brannigan's quarters were beyond the kitchen. He

knew she would finish cleaning up the kitchen now that he had eaten, and then would retire for the night. Two years earlier, when she began working for him, he had had her sitting room and bedroom made almost soundproof when he discovered that she loved to play her TV so loud he could hear it in the living room. He had told her, at the time, that he was adding more insulation to keep out the cold.

The sun set, and the room grew dark. But still, he waited.

His phone buzzed several times, but it was Richie, and he didn't answer. He only wanted to hear from one person. But she wasn't calling.

He didn't quite know when he realized he was in love with Salma. He knew from the beginning that she wouldn't leave her husband. She had a child, Adam, and her father was completely dependent on Gebran for his job, his income. Also, Gebran adored his son, much more than he ever cared for Salma. She knew Gebran would never allow her to leave him and take Adam with her. And she wouldn't leave without her son.

Shay remembered Salma telling him how, when she heard that she and her father were coming to America, she had dreamed of what a wonderful adventure it would be. She had hopes for a handsome husband and a beautiful home like she'd seen in the movies. And then she met Gebran. He wasn't handsome, and looked older than his years, overweight, and balding. But she didn't care that much about his looks if he was a good man, and a good husband. She quickly realized that Gebran was devoted to his mother, put up with his brother, Yussef, and not only supported both, but both lived with him.

When Salma moved in as his wife, she was less than second-class; she was third. Being the youngest one, it was up to her to take over the housework while Fairuz took over giving orders. Salma soon came to hate her life and everything about it, everything except her son.

Yussef had resented her presence as well as her marriage to his brother. He often said things implying she should welcome his advances—that he was younger, handsomer, and more virile than his workaholic brother. She found his interest in her repulsive, but she never said anything to Gebran.

When Adam was born, Yussef moved out of the house to an apartment near his job in San Mateo. Yussef's room became Adam's. Salma was glad to see him go, but him being out of the house didn't make life with Fairuz any easier. Fairuz quickly added Salma's deficiency as a mother to all her other faults.

Salma often said that only when she was with Shay did she remember the happy young woman she had once been, the one who had hoped for so much more from life than she had found.

The living room was completely dark when the doorbell rang. He lit the lamp and, having lost all track of time, glanced at his watch. It was 1:30 in the morning.

Would Salma come this late?

He went down the stairs to a massive front door with stained glass insets. He was normally cautious, but tonight he threw caution to the wind and threw open the door.

Salma stood on the front stoop.

24

Rebecca lay on the bed in Richie's guest room, thinking of all that happened that day.

Earlier that evening, Sutter had phoned to say Salma was gone, and that Gebran was all but apoplectic about her disappearance, saying Sutter and Rebecca had driven her to run away because of their threats, intimidation, and harassment.

Eastwood issued a warrant for Salma Najjar's arrest based on her attack on Rebecca, but Sutter said Rebecca needed to get back to work as soon as she could to keep things moving. She thanked him for stepping in and said she would be at work the next morning.

Or, so she hoped. She kept drifting in and out of sleep as something about the case kept niggling at her, but she couldn't quite put her finger on it.

She wondered if she should just get up. Nearby, Richie sat sound asleep in an easy chair. She couldn't help but smile. So much for being the great protector who would keep her awake if she fell asleep in her potentially concussed state.

Sometimes, simply looking at him caused her to realize she really had fallen in love with him despite her best efforts not to.

Yet so many barriers stood in the way of their happiness—not the least of which being the 'ideal' that was Isabella—it made her heart hurt.

She tried not to think about all that and turned her thoughts instead to the Najjar family. Salma had to be Yussef's killer. That was the only logical reason for her to have lashed out and run away.

But the motive for the killing, Rebecca didn't yet know. That would involve talking to Salma and trying to make sense out of it all.

Rebecca kept trying to put the pieces together. The answer seemed to be just past the recesses of her thoughts. But then, her eyes shut and she fell asleep.

~

Shay stepped to one side as Salma entered the house. His heart beat too hard and too fast, and he didn't want to look at her; he didn't think he could bear it. Yet, he couldn't help but notice each tiny movement of the small muscles surrounding her lips, the faintest flicker of her eyelashes, the small lift of her fingers.

He quickly turned and marched ahead of her up the stairs to his apartment. She followed.

He waited in silence as she entered the room. Only one lamp was lit.

He held himself stiffly and took a couple of deep breaths before he found his voice. "Why didn't you tell me about the girl?"

Salma slowly walked over to the sofa, lightly running her fingertips over the shade of the table lamp and atop the cherry wood end table beside it. "This home is a far cry from the shabby studio you used to rent." She faced him with a hint of a smile, even as her eyes were desolate.

At her words, memories rocked him like a blow to the chest,

and his head swam with visions of her in his arms, of their afternoons in his tiny one-room place. His willful eyes traveled over the soft outlines of her body, and he couldn't help but remember how well he knew every contour, every promise it held.

He said nothing. All he knew was that she was every bit as beautiful and desirable now as she had been then. Maybe more so.

She sat down on the sofa and folded long, graceful hands on her lap. "So, you've seen her?"

He moved closer, his mouth firm. "You should have told me."

"I'm sorry, but I..." She squared her shoulders. "You know how it was with Gebran. I didn't know for sure you were the father until I saw her fair skin and, of course, her eyes. But a baby's eyes often change color, you know. In any case, when they didn't, I had to convince Gebran that someone far back in my family had eyes that color."

"He believed you?"

"Who knows? He said he did. My father backed me, saying his grandmother had blue eyes and light hair, and that everyone had remarked about them."

"But once you knew, why didn't you tell me?" Arms folded, he glared down at her.

Her face hardened. "Didn't we agree not to meet ever again?" She was now matching his cold anger with her own. "To never see each other again? To try to forget?"

He shook his head. "That was no reason—"

"What good would it have done?" She shouted the words, standing and facing him. But then her voice broke, and all pretext vanished. "It would only cause more heartache for everyone, including you. I know your heart, I know how you would feel. How you *do* feel now. But you knew I couldn't walk away from my family. I would have had to leave my son, and my father would have become destitute, and Gebran might have become violent again." She shut her eyes as if to block Shay from her sight, and then sat, angled so that her back was toward him, her hands gripping the arm of the sofa.

He sat beside her. "Back then, I couldn't have helped out much," he admitted. He couldn't see her face which made it easier to speak. "After you left, I vowed I would never be in that situation again, where I couldn't help the one person who meant everything in the world to me. I developed a plan to get 'rich'—and I did. I can help you this time. It won't be like before. I have money. A lot of money."

She shook her head, and after a while, she turned to him again. "I was late getting here because I had to speak to my father. He had to understand, and to help. He worked out what would be best for everyone—and that includes you. He's a good man, Shay, a wise, loving man, as you know."

The way she was looking at him, he was almost afraid to ask. "What's the plan?"

"I've got to leave, and I've got to go alone. I have no choice, and I can't bring children with me, given the life I'll be living. I want to stay with them, and, were such a thing possible in this world, with you. But I can't. I'm here to beg you to help me get away."

"I don't understand!" he insisted. "What happened was self-defense! We'll get someone to believe that."

"If we couldn't prove it nine years ago, how do we prove it now? Gebran has even more power in the community than he did back then. His friends will all say Yussef was a good man—that he wouldn't do anything to me, that I'm making up the story, and that's why I didn't go to the police at the time. If he truly had tried to raped me, I should have been able to prove it. Gebran would say I didn't go to the police because there was no proof his brother was a monster. That's what he would say, and I have no way, now, to prove that he's wrong."

Shay caught her hands. "You're not alone anymore. We'll take the children and go together, or at least take our daughter."

She freed herself from his grip. "How long could we hide? And what kind of life would it be for them? Or for you? Maybe in time I can let you know where I am, and perhaps see them, and you, once more."

"But you're innocent," he insisted.

"What if I'm not?" she whispered. "You said you've changed over the years. Well, so have I. Please, Shay. I'm begging you. If you want to help, don't make me face the law with this, help me get away. I'm scared, and I don't want my children to see me this way." She struggled to hold back tears. "Please, if you ever cared about me at all."

He could never deny her anything. That was always the problem. It had become second nature to him to do what she wanted, and to protect her, whatever the cost. And that was why he was afraid to get involved again. Strong, tough, HIT-man, afraid his heart would run away with his reason. It had once, and now it was again.

"Wait here while I make some phone calls." When she nodded, he walked into his study and shut the door.

25

Richie woke to find Rebecca standing over him, shaking his shoulder.

"Richie, time to go to bed," she said. "You're going to be miserable in the morning if you sleep scrunched up in this chair all night."

His neck had a crook in it, and he blinked a few times before he sat up. Then, with a groan, he bent forward at the waist, his head hanging forward sleepily. "I'm supposed to be keeping you awake," he mumbled.

"Like you'll be a big help. Or maybe you plan to keep me awake with your snoring?"

"I never snore."

"And buzz saws are quiet, too."

He slowly rose to his feet. "I am tired," he admitted. "Okay, let's go."

"Go?"

"To my room. You don't think I'm leaving you alone tonight."

She went with him and slipped under the covers as he undressed. But by the time he got into bed, he was wide awake.

"How does your head feel?" he asked, leaning over her. His hand gently traced a path from the side of her face to her neck, her shoulder, lower...

"I've got the headache from hell, but I think it'll be okay soon."

His hand stilled. "A headache?" Richie rolled onto his back. "And we aren't even married."

"Married? Where did that come from?"

"I know how you women think."

"Oh, you do, Mr. Smart Alec Know-it-all. This time, you're quite wrong!"

"I only know what my buddies tell me about married life, and it ain't pretty!"

"Not to worry. It's nothing you'll ever find out about if you keep talking this way."

"*If?*" Richie propped himself up on an elbow to look at her, with a roguish smile. "That sounds like progress."

All of a sudden, Rebecca sat bolt upright, nearly knocking Richie onto his back once more. "She's at Shay's house."

"What? Who?"

"Salma. What time is it?"

Richie picked up his watch from the nightstand. "It's—oh, my God—it's six in the morning. I've never been awake at six in the morning. Go back to sleep."

"I can't. If she's there... They had some kind of history, that's obvious, but what if Shay doesn't know she's killed two people? He could be in danger!"

"Shay? No way."

"Yes! We've got to get over there right now."

~

Shay didn't want to touch her, but he seemed unable to keep his hands from reaching out to hold her narrow shoulders, and then brush her hair back from her face. Its angles were sharper than when she was in her twenties, deeper and more interesting, while her eyes had a sadness and desperation he hadn't seen before. Still, it was as if all the years they had been apart vanished into nothing.

He dropped his hands and stepped back. "I can get a private plane for you. It'll take you close to Toronto. Once you're in Canada, money and papers will be waiting. Canada is bringing in a lot of refugees, and I suspect all their paperwork, including that from Lebanon, is irregular. All you need to do is find a way to blend in."

She gave a wan smile. "Don't be too American, in other words."

"That's right."

"There's one more thing," she said. "When I leave, I worry about Hannah."

The name was like a stab to his heart. "Hannah? That's her name?"

Salma nodded. "Gebran may make her life miserable when I'm gone. I can't be sure… I shouldn't speak badly of him, he has always been a good provider, a hard worker. And even though he always suspected something, he never spoke against me or Hannah. At the same time, he's rather … cold to her." She paused. "My father knows and understands what happened, but at some point, he might need your help."

"Of course I'll help him. Whatever he needs. And … and Hannah, too."

"Keep watch over her, please. One day I hope you'll meet our daughter. She's wonderful—and a bit strange, like her father." As Salma studied his face, her hand lifted slightly, and he thought—hoped—she would reach for him. But she let it drop back to her side. "She's so smart, it sometimes frightens me. She is truly your child."

He felt as if he were shattering inside. "And your son?" he whispered.

"Adam will be fine with Gebran."

Shay shook his head. "I'm sorry about so much."

"Don't be. Don't ever be." She looked at him with those beautiful deep brown eyes. "I was cruel to you when I left you, but I never stopped loving you. Every minute. Every day."

"Salma." Her name was a prayer on his lips. He wished he could hate her—hate her for the smiles she never gave him, for the family they would never have, not even when she had borne his only child. He wished he could hate her for all the years that would never be theirs, and for the empty despair he felt whenever he thought of her. But that was a wish that would never come true.

She stood. "I have to go. I have things I must do before I can leave—mainly writing out some information about the children for my father. I have to do it alone, or I know I'll forget. But, as I said, he understands and will help."

"Wait." Shay stepped into his study, and when he returned, he handed her some cash and a burner phone. "Call the number on the phone when you're ready to leave. I'll let you know where to meet the driver who'll take you to a private plane."

"Thank you."

He nodded. She gave him a quick kiss, then turned to go. But he caught her wrist.

She stared at him, and then their lips met as he pulled her close, holding her tight, not wanting to ever let go. And she held him the same way. For that moment, that brief moment, time stopped, and he allowed himself to remember how it once felt to love, and to be loved.

But then, she broke his hold and left the house.

He watched her drive away, and when he could no longer

see her, he shut the door and returned to his private, terrible solitude.

∼

Richie drove Rebecca to pick up her car which was still outside the Najjar home in the Oceanview area. He couldn't believe how early she'd gotten him up, but at least he was relieved that she seemed fine and her headache was lessening.

He then drove to Shay's house, with Rebecca following in her SUV.

Richie rang the doorbell and Mrs. Brannigan opened the door.

"Oh, my," she said, looking at Richie, "the world really has spun off its axis. I didn't think you ever saw the light of early morning. Sort of like that Count Dracula, himself, come to think of it."

"Very funny. And, this is Inspector Rebecca Mayfield," Richie said as they stepped into the foyer.

"Rebecca, Mrs. Brannigan. Shay thinks she's his housekeeper, but really she's the one who keeps him."

"Posh, Richie! You're too cheeky by half. And it's nice to meet you, Inspector Mayfield," Mrs. Brannigan said. "Give me a moment while I see if—"

"It's okay," Shay said as he walked down the stairs. "I've been expecting them."

Mrs. Brannigan gave him a strange look, one eyebrow lifted, and then went back up to his apartment.

"I'm here to arrest Salma," Rebecca said. "I hope you won't try to interfere."

"She's not here," he said.

"But you've seen her," Rebecca stated.

Shay nodded. "She told me what happened."

"What did you do?" Rebecca asked.

"I did what I've always done," Shay said. His body blocked the stairs up to his living area.

As Rebecca eyed the stairway, Richie spoke up. "You helped her?"

Shay folded his arms. "Maybe I've done nothing."

"Or, you helped her," Richie repeated.

"She's not some innocent person who needs protection," Rebecca said. "I believe she's killed two people."

"Two?" Shay looked stunned.

"Yussef and her mother-in-law, Fairuz Najjar."

His lips tightened. "I have nothing to say."

"Where is she?" Rebecca demanded. "You can't hide her. That puts you in legal jeopardy."

"I'm not hiding her," he said. "You can search my house. Search everywhere you want ... with a warrant, of course."

"I can bring you in and demand answers." She spat out the words.

"Try it." His tone was low, threatening.

"Stop!" Richie insisted. "This has gone far enough. If Shay says he's not hiding her here, he's not. That doesn't mean he hasn't given her money"—he studied Shay closely as he added—"fake id's, maybe a plane, and heaven-only-knows what else to help her escape. In fact, I suspect that's what he did. But proving it will be another story, especially if we can't find her."

"I will find her." Rebecca's eyes bored into Shay's.

"I won't let you," Shay stated.

"You'll have no choice."

Shay pulled open the front door. "I have nothing more to say to you."

Richie faced Rebecca. "Go," he said softly. "Please."

She looked from him to Shay. "Shay, I'm sorry, but eventually you will need to tell me where she's gone. The woman is dangerous."

26

In Shay's living room, Richie sat on the sofa and stared at his friend. "Whenever you're ready," he said gently. "I can't help you if I don't know what's going on."

"It's a long story," Shay said.

"Given how ungodly early it is, we've got all day—a long, long time."

Mrs. Brannigan walked into the living room carrying a tray with coffee, Irish soda bread, and a variety of jams and lemon curd. "If I'd known Mr. Tate was going to be entertaining this morning, I'd have made something fancy for you, but this will have to do."

"Thanks," Shay said, pouring them both some coffee. He sat in a wingback chair across from Richie.

"That helps," Richie said, after taking a sip of coffee and buttering some bread. "Anytime you're ready."

"I don't like to talk about myself," Shay said.

"No, really? That's a news bulletin. In case you didn't know it, you're more close-mouthed than anyone I've ever met. Now, why are you helping a woman Rebecca thinks has murdered two people?"

Shay put down his coffee cup and walked over to the window. He kept his back to Richie, looking out at the street and at the sun coming up over a tree-filled park in the distance. His words were soft. "There's a number of reasons."

"I guessed that."

Shay faced him, his face bleaker and more troubled than Richie had ever seen it. "And," Shay all but whispered, "she's the mother of my daughter."

Richie didn't say a word as the full impact of Shay's words struck. He put down the bread. "My God."

Shay's jaw was tight. "It'll be hard enough on the girl that her mother's gone, without hearing that she's a murderer as well."

Richie rose and took a step toward Shay. "Hold on, here. Out of the blue, you announce you have a daughter? Why have you kept this a secret?"

"I didn't. Not the way you think. I only learned about her a few days ago."

Richie studied Shay's face looking for bitterness, relief, or anything that would help him understand what his friend was thinking, how he was processing all this. He saw nothing but rigidity and stoicism.

"Good Christ." Richie went back to the sofa. Shay followed and sat again on the wingback chair. The two friends just stared at each other a long moment, shaking their heads. Richie could see that Shay was even more stunned by this turn of events than he was.

"Okay," Richie said after a while. "We've got to figure this out like two logical human beings."

"It's okay. I can handle it."

"Shay, you can't do everything by yourself. There are other people involved now. Including a child. So ... so how old is she?"

Shay swallowed hard. "Eight."

"Her name?"

Shay's breath seemed to quicken. "Hannah."

"That's a nice name," Richie said, then thought a moment. "Look, maybe I shouldn't bring this up, but the woman has a husband. Are you sure—?"

"I saw her," Shay said. "Even before Salma told me, I knew. I was sure."

Richie rubbed his temple. "God, I still don't believe it. You, of all people." As he looked at Shay, his mouth slowly turned into a smile. "I mean, wow."

"What are you saying?" Shay demanded.

Richie's grin widened. "Nothing, nothing at all. All I can say, Big Daddy, is you've helped me help others. Now, it's my turn to help you. But first, I need to know the story, the whole story this time."

Shay shut his eyes a moment. "That's fair," he said, then nodded. "But where to start? I think ... it might have been all the time I spent in the Middle East helped me understand Salma Najjar. She left Lebanon behind, but still lives by the rules of its culture, not ours. She married Gebran for the sake of her father, in fact. Gebran had money and a business. What he didn't have was a wife. When we met she was unhappy, and as a result open, and perhaps vulnerable. Too vulnerable.

"I guess it was easy for her to fall for a man who had no ties, and no family to speak of. She told me that when she first came to this country, she had high hopes for her future, but she quickly realized that, even here, she couldn't break her traditions and family obligations. She simply didn't know how. She would say how much she envied me my complete freedom. She never understood that being completely alone could be its own form of punishment.

"Also, as much as I understood her because of my experiences, because of hers, she understood me. In Lebanon she had seen what fighting and killing can do to a man. Do you know how many Americans, particularly women, simply have no understanding at all about that way of life or how it affects a person? Even you, Richie—you're a friend—but if I told you some of the things I've seen and done, you'd walk out of here and never look back."

"No, I wouldn't."

"Let's hope I never have to test that," Shay said.

"I trust you, and I do hope you do me." Richie waited a moment, then asked, "So, what happened with you and Salma?"

"We kept seeing each other despite her marriage. We saw each other for over six months. It went on long enough we became complacent, took chances. Particularly the one time Gebran went out of town, overnight, for some dry-cleaner franchiser meeting.

"The next day, she called in a panic. Her brother-in-law had seen her with me that morning and then followed her to her husband's dry cleaners where she had to relieve her father for a doctor's appointment. Yussef waited until her father, Zair, had gone, and then he entered the shop.

"He confronted her—told her he'd tell his brother about her affair. She'd be divorced and her father out of work. She would never see her boy again. He even threatened her with deportation. I know that when they were in Lebanon, her father was afraid for his life. She feared he'd be killed if they were sent back.

"She begged Yussef not to tell Gebran. He told her what she needed to do to 'win' his silence, and then he locked the shop door. She grabbed the gun kept under the till in case of robbery, and as soon as she got the chance, she shot him."

"So she killed him," Richie murmured.

Shay nodded. "When her father arrived back from the doctor's, he saw what had happened. The two put Yussef's body in the trunk of her father's car, and cleaned up the shop so that when Gebran returned to the city, he'd think they had cleaned the carpets and all, with no suspicion of what had actually happened there.

"After that, Salma called me. In the middle of the night, her father and I met and moved Yussef's body into the park, to such a remote area I thought there was no chance he'd be found. I was right, for nine years."

"What happened between you and Salma after the killing?" Richie asked.

"I saw her two times, then not again until now."

"That's hard to believe."

"Too much had happened. First, we had the problem of Yussef's disappearance. I learned a big bank robbery took place in the city and the robbers had cleanly gotten away. I found a map of the bank's interior and gave it to her. When Gebran and Fairuz realized Yussef had disappeared, she told him she had overheard him having a strange conversation on the phone, and watched him throw some papers away. She then gave them the map of the bank.

"As much as Gebran and Fairuz didn't want to believe Yussef would rob a bank, once confronted with Salma's evidence, they feared if he were linked to the robbery, the government might go after all of them, possibly deport them. It was a chance they didn't dare to take. And, they had no reason *not* to believe Salma. Yussef was always a bit weird, about everything. As a result, they decided to tell the police Yussef had left the country."

"You covered everything for her," Richie said.

"So I'd thought," Shay said.

"How could you two split up after all that?"

Shay's mouth contorted into what was almost a smirk—wry, dismayed, and yet sad. "We fantasized about running away, even leaving the country. But it was just a fantasy. I'd just quit the military and was still pretty raw. And broke. If we ran, we'd have to do it with nothing. I could try to hide Salma and her child, but what if I failed?" He paused, then continued in a hushed voice. "The more I thought about it, the more I realized that for her to disappear would have caused the police to suspect foul play—they'd have dug further into Yussef's disappearance as well as her own. Just as Yussef saw us together, others might have as well. It was too much of a chance to take. If she was caught, we had no money for good lawyers. No proof that what she did was self-defense. The chance was great that she would spend years in prison. I couldn't let her take that chance. I couldn't let her run."

"Did she agree?"

"No." The word was cold, clipped. "She said she didn't care, and that since I had also killed people, I should understand. I continued to say no, that she had to stick to the bank robbery story, and stay with Gebran."

Richie nodded. "And, in the end, that's what she did?"

Shay walked over to the window and kept his back to Richie as he continued. "She was furious at me for not going along with her plan to run away together. Finally, she said she never loved me anyway—that no woman could. She said I'm too scary for anyone to really love, and far too crazy. She had thought I was brave enough to help her get away from her ugly life, but she'd been wrong.

"I tried to say she was lying, striking back at me. But she doubled-down. She said that for the first time since she met me, she was telling me the truth."

"God," Richie whispered, heartsick for his friend.

Shay folded his arms and faced Richie once more. "I don't think even He could help."

"So which is the truth? That she loved you, or she used to?"

He shook his head. "I wasn't sure until last night."

Richie waited, but Shay didn't tell him which version of Salma he had decided was real. Richie knew he shouldn't have expected an answer, but for Shay's sake, he hoped it was the woman who loved him, not the bitter one that he had made walk away.

"And now," Richie said, "she's come back to you for help."

He nodded. "We talked about Hannah, mostly. I won't tell you that I did anything to help Salma, because you'd feel obligated to tell Mayfield. All I can say is that Salma found a way to get her wish to run off. And she did. Finally."

27

Rebecca wasn't pleased at Richie asking her to leave Shay's house, but she could tell there would be no meeting of the minds that day, and she really didn't want to create a permanent rift between herself and Shay. She hoped, given enough time, she would be able to talk to him about Salma without feeling like a participant in a cage match.

She drove to A-1 Cleaners, the shop owned by Gebran Najjar. She wanted to see what it looked like, as well as to question Salma's father.

A sign on the door said the shop was closed due to a death in the family, but if someone needed to pick up their dry cleaning, to ring the bell during the shop's normal hours, 8 a.m. to 7 p.m. She rang the bell.

An older man answered. "Are you Salma Najjar's father?" she asked, showing her badge.

"Yes." He looked scared as she entered the shop and she couldn't help but think he feared she had bad news about Salma.

"I'm Inspector Mayfield, Homicide. I'm looking into the death of Yussef Najjar. Your name is?"

Relief seemed to wash over him. She wasn't used to people feeling relieved around her. It was rather nice, actually. "Zair Lahoud," he said. Despite what Gebran had told her about his father-in-law's English ability, the man seemed to have no trouble understanding her. He stepped behind the counter and she remained on the customer's side.

"I'm sorry to say, Mr. Lahoud, that Yussef Najjar's death is being looked as a murder investigation," she told him. "I'd like to know if you saw anything suspicious around the time of Mr. Najjar's disappearance."

"I never saw anything suspicious. No, never." He vigorously shook his head. "It was a long time ago. And, please, call me Zair."

"Thank you," she murmured, caught off guard by his friendly demeanor. "Did you believe Yussef had gone back to Lebanon?"

Zair waggled his head in a sort of "maybe yes, maybe no" manner. "Of course, I did. Although, I didn't understand why he would want to go to such a place."

"I've heard there were some men who fought with Yussef, and that they might have been friends with Gebran."

"Hmm." Zair looked puzzled. "I don't remember Gebran having any close friends back then. Or now. Or anyone fighting with Yussef."

"Did the brothers get along?"

"Of course, very well," he announced loud and clear before adding, "Although, Gebran owns a business ... and yet, he didn't want Yussef to work for him. So maybe something was wrong between them."

"Why didn't he want Yussef working for him?"

"I don't know. Maybe he didn't trust Yussef. You should ask him, not me."

"I have," Rebecca said. "What did you think of Yussef?"

Zair shrugged. "Everyone liked him. He was a nice fellow, of course. Although, he was not very happy. I didn't like being around him."

"How well do you get along with Gebran?" she asked.

"Very well, of course! Although, he is my boss, so sometimes that can be difficult. Mostly, I try to keep quiet, keep him happy." Zair shrugged again.

Rebecca was finding this entire conversation peculiar—the emphatically positive answers followed by an "although" with a negative revelation. She knew which part of the answers to believe.

"Are you close to Salma?" she asked, finally broaching the subject that most interested her.

"Oh, yes. She is a good daughter, a good mother, and wife."

"Did she have a good relationship with Yussef?"

"With Yussef? I suspect so. I don't know."

"What about her mother-in-law, Fairuz? Did the two get along?"

For the first time, Zair stopped smiling. "Fairuz was not an easy woman. Very bossy." He sighed. "Salma is a good girl. She didn't fight with her, but tried to keep peace in the family."

"I see. And has your daughter returned home yet?" Rebecca asked.

Zair looked stricken, then dropped his gaze. "Returned home? I don't understand."

"You know she's gone. Gebran contacted you looking for her," she said. Zair blanched at her words. She had only been guessing, but was pretty sure it was a good guess.

"Don't lie to me," she warned. "Where is Salma?"

"I don't know."

"Where might she be hiding?"

"Truly, I have no idea." He kept his eyes downcast. He was most likely lying, and would continue to do so as long as he believed his lies would keep his daughter safe.

Rebecca changed her tactic. "What about the children? Who's taking care of them?"

"Gebran will do it until she returns."

"You think she'll return?"

He looked at her directly. "She was frightened—by you! Or, that is what Gebran told me. But she has done nothing wrong, so she will return to her home and children. It would kill her not to see them."

Rebecca turned away, hoping the man's emotions would calm a bit. As she looked around the shop, she noticed a camera and quite a few locks on the door. "This isn't the safest area," she said, facing him again. "What kind of protection do you keep here?"

Zair blanched. "We call the police, of course."

"Although..." Rebecca prompted, "until they arrive, you must have something..."

He looked quite uncomfortable. "I don't—"

"Show me."

"But—"

"Where is it?" she asked sternly.

He bit his bottom lip, then walked over to the cash register and reached under it. He held up a Glock with two fingers, making it clear he wasn't threatening her. "Is this what you want?"

"Is it registered?" she asked.

"I'm sure it is. Gebran's mother bought it when the boys were young. Fairuz was alone, and the neighborhood wasn't so good twenty years ago. She was a tough woman."

Rebecca took the gun and placed it in a plastic dry-cleaning bag. "It needs to be tested. Depending on the results, it will either be quickly returned to you or put into evidence." She handed him her card. "Call me if you think of anything to add, or if you hear from your daughter."

"Yes," he said with a slight bow of the head. "Thank you, Miss Inspector. I will, of course."

And pigs fly, she thought as she walked out the door.

~

Rebecca took the gun to the Crime Scene Investigations Unit laboratory to be tested. They had possession of the bullet found in the dirt near Yussef Najjar's body, but they hadn't been able to match it up to any known handguns.

As the CSIU checked the Glock 26 against the bullet, Rebecca looked up the Dealers Record of Purchase, and found that Fairuz Najjar had lawfully purchased the gun. It surprised her that the woman had bought herself a gun—it wasn't a common thing for women in San Francisco to do.

"You did it," Inspector Alejandro Pacheco called out as Rebecca reentered CSIU. "The bullet came from this gun."

"Thanks, Al," Rebecca said. "I appreciate your fast action."

Back in Homicide, Rebecca sat back and tried to think this through. She understood there must have been a strong relationship between Shay and Salma, and she could understand Shay trying to mislead her investigation away from Salma because of it. She could also see Gebran being involved in a bad way in this situation. Everyone praised his work ethic, but no one praised him as a loving, supporting husband.

Yussef, on the other hand, had worked in a carpet warehouse in San Mateo. He lived in a tiny apartment and drove an old car. Nothing of interest or note had shown up in his finances.

Why, then, did anyone want him dead?

28

Since the gun used in Yussef's murder had been accessible to all members of the Najjar household, and since the family had lied to the police when they said he went to Lebanon, Rebecca and Sutter were granted a warrant to search Gebran Najjar's home and business. In addition, the fact that Salma Najjar was the last person to have seen Fairuz alive, had attacked Rebecca when she tried to question her, and now seemed to have disappeared, Lt. Eastwood also authorized an autopsy on Fairuz.

Evelyn quickly handled it. She found that Fairuz had been smothered. Her mouth, throat and nasal passages contained particles common in the pillows and pillowcases used by the nursing home.

Rebecca now had the proof she needed for a convincing argument that Salma had in fact killed her. But why? And did that mean she also had killed Yussef? There was some key, some element, she was missing. But what?

Rebecca was more troubled than ever by Shay's involvement. She had her differences with him, but she couldn't imagine him as someone willing to lie to protect a murderer. In her experience, Shay simply didn't lie. But now, she was certain he had. Was it love? Loyalty? Or something more?

Rebecca and Sutter went with a team of CSI detectives to the Najjar home to search for anything that might point to Yussef or Fairuz's murders, or to a motive for the murders. As the team went through the house, Sutter asked Gebran if he had heard anything from Salma. He swore he still didn't know where his wife was and had heard nothing.

"Have you asked your children? Maybe they have some idea," Rebecca suggested. "They're old enough. They might have heard something."

"The boy is twelve, the girl eight." Gebran said. He didn't look happy about her request, but after a moment stated, "I'll get them."

He had the two children march into the room and stand before the two detectives. They seemed frightened, and both kept their heads bowed.

"Do you know where your mother is?" Gebran asked.

They shook their heads.

"Did you hear her say anything about where she was going?" he asked.

Same response.

"What are their names?" Rebecca asked Gebran.

"Adam and Hannah."

Rebecca faced the boy. "Adam, when did you last see your mother?"

"In the morning when I went to school," he murmured, still staring at the floor.

"Hannah, what about you?"

The girl looked up at Rebecca. Rebecca couldn't help but stare a moment at her large blue eyes ... blue with a hint of lavender circling the irises. She had seen eyes like that before, and suddenly everything made sense to her.

"I last saw my mother when she walked me to the bus stop,"

Hannah said. Her voice was tiny but her words distinct. "She patted my head like she always does, and told me to be sure to eat the cookies she packed in my lunch, and that she gave me an extra one so I could share it with Bethany, if I wanted. But only if I wanted." Tears filled the girl's eyes, and this time she scarcely whispered. "I haven't seen her since then."

Rebecca swallowed hard, and her words were also merely a whisper. "I see, thank you." With that, still somewhat shaken by her realization about Hannah, Rebecca looked up at Gebran. "While we conduct the search, you might want to take the children out for ice cream or something. We'll lock up when we're done."

"I guess so." He glared at her, Sutter, and the children, then folded his arms. "Get your coats," he said gruffly. "We're going out."

~

As soon as a Rebecca could get away from Homicide that evening, she called Richie to make sure he was home, and said, "Wait for me there." She stopped only long enough to pick up her phoned-in order from their favorite Chinese restaurant. She realized that thinking in terms of "their" favorite rather than "his" or "hers" was another of those big steps that she kept saying she wasn't ready to take, but at the same time, it felt good.

She also felt good about the way Richie had stepped up to take care of her when Salma Najjar knocked her down the stairs. She could have been badly hurt or even killed. Nice woman you found for yourself, Shay, she thought. Given the friendships involved, this situation was a nightmare.

"Here I am," she said waving the bags of food when Richie opened his front door.

"Not a minute too soon. It smells great!" Richie said. They

spread the food out on the kitchen table, and Richie made a pot of oolong tea.

She didn't want to upset his dinner too much, but he had only taken a couple of bites when she said, "I can't hold it in a minute longer. I found out why Shay is so willing to help Salma Najjar."

"You did?" Richie asked nonchalantly.

She nodded. "Salma's daughter is his child. I've never seen anyone with eyes quite like his until this afternoon. They were startling. Also, something about the shape of her mouth reminded me of Shay. But then the kicker was when I asked a simple little question, she gave me a such a precise answer, she sounded exactly like guess who? And she's only eight."

Richie smiled broadly at her tale. "So she really is his kid."

"Don't tell me you already knew?"

"I just found out this morning. Shay just found out himself. By the way, I'm pretty sure he helped Salma get out of the country, although he'd never admit it."

Rebecca nearly choked on a bite of eggroll. "He helped her? That's illegal. She's wanted for murder!"

"I didn't say he helped her, and neither did he. Let's say he assumes she's out of the country. How's that? She's not his problem, after all. He had nothing to do with any of this."

"Richie, you can't just—"

"I'm not doing a thing. In fact, Shay's assumption could be wrong. Maybe you and Sutter should continue to look for her. After all, what does Shay know about any of this?" His blathering told her he knew a lot more than he would ever admit, but she had no proof. "Intuition" wasn't a legal finding.

"Anyway, I'll tell you what I do know," he continued. "I know that if Shay thinks she's a good woman and doesn't deserve to be jailed for the rest of her life, I'll go along with him."

"It's not for you or Shay to decide."

"I'm just saying." He twirled some chow mein noodles in a circle as if they were spaghetti then picked them up with his chopsticks. She tried not to let him distract her.

"I have no choice but to look for her," Rebecca insisted. "And if I find her, to arrest her, no matter what you, Shay, or even I might think about the situation."

Richie put down the chopsticks. "Right. And there are consequences for murdering someone. Horrible consequences." His tone was hard as ice. "Shay understands that as well. I only hope, Rebecca, it doesn't come to what you're suggesting."

They continued with dinner, although to Rebecca, at this point it could have been cardboard.

29

Rebecca ran her hands through her hair as she sat at her desk the next morning and tried to figure out what to do next about Salma Najjar. She was in the wind and Rebecca knew why.

Last evening, Richie had told her the story of Shay and Salma's affair, but nothing about Yussef's murder. Still, Rebecca was quite certain that Salma was the killer, and that the men who loved her had done all they could to protect her. If she ever did establish Salma as Yussef's murderer, she feared she could arrest not only Salma, but her father and Shay as accomplices.

Rebecca cared about Shay, and the thought that he had a daughter he hadn't known about added to the sympathy she felt for him. Given his quirky, loner personality, she couldn't imagine how he was handling such news. She also wondered how he was going to cope with his daughter being raised by someone like Gebran Najjar, who might have serious doubts about the girl's paternity if information about Shay's involvement became known.

That poor child.

After speaking with Lt. Eastwood, an all-points bulletin had been issued on Salma, and the Najjar home, her father's apartment, Shay's house, and the dry cleaning shop were all under surveillance. All Rebecca could do was wait.

In the meantime, she realized Shay must have been so caught up in his own situation he hadn't had much time to look into Richie's. She found it ironic that Richie was trying to come up with who was responsible, if anyone, for the death of a woman he loved, and at the same time, his best friend was trying to work out how to help a woman he loved escape the ramifications of killing others.

Rebecca felt caught in the middle. There was nothing she could do to help Shay. If anything, her involvement only made it worse.

As she was pondering this she received a call from Rachel Swann, a deputy sheriff in Phoenix, Arizona.

A few days earlier, as Rebecca tried to track down Isabella's assistant loan officer, Cory Egerton, she discovered the name was an alias. His real name was Colin Sigurdson, and Sigurdson was incarcerated in the Arizona State Prison for second-degree murder in the killing of his partner in a scheme to blackmail several rich businessmen. Rebecca had immediately contacted Deputy Swann, saying she was working on a cold case and the man she knew as Cory Egerton potentially had some information she needed. Swann had agreed to allow Rebecca to hold a meeting with the prisoner as long as he had an attorney present. Rebecca had flown to Phoenix, but Egerton had refused to cooperate.

Now, however, Deputy Swann was calling with new information.

"I couldn't help but feel," Swann said, "that the prisoner you call Cory Egerton knows a lot more than he was saying the last time you were here. Right now, I think there may have a way to get him to talk to you. He's been giving us trouble and has had a number of privileges taken away. But he loves the Internet, and

I think if he cooperates with you, we might just let him go use a computer again. He's no dummy, Inspector, and I know he enjoys seeing what's going on in the world even if it's only on the limited Internet access that we allow prisoners."

"That's good news," Rebecca said. "Whatever we can use that might get him to talk is fine with me. I'll do what I can to catch the next plane out. Thanks for letting me know."

She found a nonstop, two-hour flight from San Francisco International to Phoenix leaving in about ninety minutes, with a late night return. She dashed out of Homicide saying only she'd be away most of the day, but back that night. Thanks to BART trains and TSA pre-check, she made the flight.

At the Phoenix airport, she rented a car and drove to the Arizona State Prison. Deputy Swann was there when she arrived and led her to an interview room where Egerton waited with a legal aid attorney at his side.

The prisoner sat slumped in the chair, handcuffs on his wrists, and a smirk on his face. He was skinny, with spiked brown hair, and looked surprisingly young.

"Well, well, well, look who's here again," Egerton said as his gaze slowly slid over Rebecca's body. "You just can't keep away from me, can you?" He chuckled. "But, it doesn't change anything. Like I told you last time, I don't have anything to say about any bank in San Francisco or any dead skank who worked there."

"And here I thought you were one of the good guys, Cory," Rebecca said as she sat down facing him. Detective Swann took the seat at her side, but sat back a bit to make it clear that this was Rebecca's show. "I thought you actually liked Isabella. After all, she did make you her assistant. I guess there was something good about you at least one time in your life."

"Or maybe it was simply that I was in the job before she got promoted ahead of me."

"Look," Rebecca said, "I don't know why you're protecting

people you obviously don't care about, but all I can say is if you tell me something about what happened four years ago in that bank with Isabella and API Holdings, I'm sure the prison officials here will be willing to give you back at least a couple of your privileges. I've been told you were a bad boy for a while and they had to punish you. But bad boys can become good if they help law enforcement. And anything you can tell me, would be a definite help."

"Are you jiving me?"

"No, not at all."

Egerton tried to fold his arms, but the handcuffs made that impossible. He glared down at them with disgust. "I'd like to get my computer privileges back," he said. "If you can make that happen, I could see myself cooperating. At least a little bit. I might not know a whole lot about it, but I might know something."

"I can do that," Rebecca said.

"Prove it."

Rebecca glanced at Deputy Swann. "Yes," Swann said.

Egerton looked at the legal aide at his side, and the woman nodded.

"Okay, I was never a part of it," Egerton said. "I want to be clear about that. But I know a money laundering scheme when I see one, and in time, so did Isabella. The way it worked was the holding company would buy a new piece of property and next thing we knew, some joker we never heard of before would come into the bank requesting a loan for that same piece of property and he'd have papers, statements, and references up the wazoo that made it so there was no way we could turn down the loan."

"So, you're saying it wasn't a loan to buy the property, it was a loan against the property? Like, say, an equity loan?" Rebecca asked.

"Exactly. I went to Isabel and told her I didn't like what I was seeing. She was glad to hear it because she had thought the same thing for a long time. Based on what I had to say, she decided to look into this holding company and the loans it was making. She found that in the past ten or twelve years that the thing had existed, no one ever repaid a single cent on those loans. Money laundering, pure and simple. She decided she was going to tell the feds about it. I'm not sure which feds. The FBI? The FDIC? I have no idea. All I knew was that if she did go that route, probably the branch where I worked, if not the whole damn bank, would be shut down. So I went to my boss. I told Skarzer what she found and what she was planning to do."

"Why didn't Isabella go to Skarzer herself?" Rebecca asked.

"Simple. She suspected he was a part of it. In fact, she suspected they all were. After all, Audrey Poole treated them all real good." Then, to Rebecca's surprise, he grinned. "In fact, if they'd offered me a cut of the action, things might have turned out differently."

"But I take it, they didn't."

"No. They were damn fools."

She let it pass. "So what happened?"

"Skarzer told me he'd get back to me soon, and after an hour or so, he called and said I needed to convince Isabella he wasn't in on the scheme, but believed her—and me—that it was happening under his nose. I was to tell her to meet him at six a.m. the next morning at a coffee shop in Sausalito. We were supposed to have a big bank meeting later that day, and he said he wanted to meet and talk to her before the meeting ever happened. So I told her about it, and she agreed. And I never saw her alive again."

"I see," Rebecca murmured. "Did you believe Skarzer's story that he wasn't involved in the scheme?"

"Hell, no!"

Rebecca drew in her breath. "Do you have any idea what

might have happened to Isabella as she drove to the Golden Gate Bridge on the way to Sausalito that morning?"

"That, I don't know," he said. "I don't know if she was in an accident, or if Skarzer, or someone else, paid someone to make Isabella run into that wall. I mean, I wouldn't have told her to go to the meeting if I thought it'd be dangerous. I really didn't. And everyone at the bank, including the managers, acted real upset by her death. Everyone liked her, and I think everyone was sorry that she had died."

"You said you contacted Skarzer to save your job. Why, then, did you quit working at the bank?"

Egerton lifted his eyebrows. "Wouldn't you, given what I knew?"

Rebecca felt sick to her stomach at hearing the story. It was what she suspected, but it would be difficult to prove. And there was always the possibility that it wasn't a bank manager who had caused Isabella's death, but Audrey Poole or one of her people. Rebecca could well imagine Skarzer being petrified by the news Egerton gave him, calling Poole, and then Poole or others she worked with took charge.

Rebecca simply didn't know, and now Poole was dead, and the holding company off the books.

She thanked Egerton and Deputy Swann for their assistance. As Egerton was escorted back to prison, Rebecca and Swann went back to Swann's office where a copy of the tape was given to Rebecca to bring back to San Francisco.

"I hope the interview helps with that cold case you've been working on," Deputy Swann said.

"It does," Rebecca replied. "It certainly does."

∽

Rebecca didn't arrive back in San Francisco until ten that night, but instead of going home, she went to Richie's club.

She was tired and frazzled, and knew she looked it, but there was no good time to deliver the news. She was halfway into the club, heading toward Richie's office, when he caught up with her. He looked as suave and debonair as always in his black suit, white shirt and black bowtie, but his expression was worried.

"What are you doing here?" he asked. "I'm always glad to see you, but you should be taking it easy. Instead, you look exhausted."

She drew in her breath. She knew this wasn't going to be easy, and she had no idea how badly he might respond. "Let's go somewhere we can talk," she said softly.

He took her arm and led her to his office, only stopping long enough to tell the bartender to send in a mai tai—her favorite drink—and a glass of ice water.

As soon as they reached his office, she faced him and handed him the cassette with the recording made in the Arizona prison. "I hope you have a tape recorder somewhere in this building," she said.

He looked at the tape, his brow furrowed. "I'll get one." He made a phone call to the nightclub's manager and asked him to bring in a cassette tape recorder ASAP. At the same time, a cocktail waitress arrived at the office with Rebecca's drinks.

"Thanks," she said to the waitress as she left the office, then turned to Richie. "I've just gotten back from Phoenix and I have news. I found Cory Egerton."

"You're kidding me," Richie said. "Not even Shay could do that."

She drank down the water quickly, and then explained how she found Egerton and how, during her second visit to Phoenix, he finally told her what he knew had happened four years earlier. As she finished with her explanation, Tommy Ginnetti, Big Caesar's manager, showed up with an old cassette tape recorder. He found an outlet to plug it in, took one look at the expressions on Richie and Rebecca's faces, and left the office with barely a word.

Richie put the tape into the machine and pressed Play.

She finished her mai tai as he listened.

When the tape ended, he sat not moving for a long moment, his lips tight, his expression bleak. "God damn," he muttered as he hit the Stop button. He took a deep breath, then faced her. "It sure as hell sounds like the boys at the bank were involved. Or,"—he stopped talking and his eyes narrowed—"or more likely someone connected with Audrey Poole did it for them. I can't see any of those bank guys having the guts to order a hit on a person, but I sure as hell can see them running to Audrey with their fears about Isabella going to the Feds. What happened to her is the kind of thing that happens to people who get in the way of big-time money launderers."

"I was wondering the same thing about Poole," Rebecca said. "I doubt those bankers have a hit man on their speed dial."

"After meeting those three," Richie said, "I don't think they had it in them. Plus, Edgerton's on tape saying Skarzer took an hour before calling him back to set up the six a.m. meeting with Isabella. I suspect he made some desperate phone calls and was told what to do. But, even if the bankers didn't actually order the hit, they're ultimately responsible. And they're going to pay."

Now, it was Rebecca's turn to pale. This was exactly what she feared. "I have friends in the FBI," she said quickly. "Please, Richie, you don't have to do anything, and I don't want you to do anything. Let me go to the FBI and let's have them handle it."

Richie's eyes smoldered. "Sure, Rebecca, I wouldn't dream of stepping on the FBI's toes."

Like hell. "I should get home," she said. "It's been a long day."

He took her in his arms. "I know this wasn't easy for you, and I can't begin to tell you how much I appreciate all you've done. You're the best."

The 'best,' yeah, just like Shay and Vito...

She stepped back from his embrace, but couldn't stop herself from reaching up and straightening the lock of hair on his forehead that had gotten mussed as he held her. "I worry about you, Richie."

"I know you do—just as I do, you," he murmured. "But I'll be fine. I promise."

As she left the office, she saw that he was already on his phone. Just before she shut the office door behind her, she heard Richie's voice saying, "Shay, I've got news."

30

Richie and Shay stood outside Ethan Nolan's Filbert Street apartment building early the next morning. It was cold; both men were miserable from not having had enough sleep, but also ready to do what needed to be done.

As soon as Nolan stepped out the door, they each took an arm and whisked the bank's data operations manager into Richie's big BMW, a car he rarely drove except to take Carmela places from time to time. Shay got in the backseat with Nolan while Richie drove to an older building in a poor, not yet gentrified area off Third Street. Nolan tried to question them, wanting to know what was going on, but neither Richie or Shay gave him any answers.

They pulled him from the car and led him through the empty building to a small room with nothing but a computer, printer and desk.

They half-shoved Nolan into the desk chair, then loomed over him.

"We know what happened to Isabella," Richie said. "We tracked down Cory Egerton, and he told us everything about Skarzer, Yamada, and you. The three of you conspired with those involved in API Holdings to launder money. When Isabella found out, it led to her death. You know what that means, Nolan. You've got to know what you're looking at now that the police are involved."

"I don't know anything," Nolan insisted. He was beyond scared, and on the verge of tears. His eyes darted back and forth between Richie and Shay, clearly remembering how easily they had been able to shove him around as if he weighed no more than a child.

"Let me show you some of the information we picked up off of Isabella's laptop." Shay tossed the paperwork he had printed out onto the desk in front of Nolan.

Nolan's eyes blinked several times and then he slowly, carefully, thumbed through the paperwork. "I've never seen any of this stuff before. I have no idea what it means. I'm just a data operations guy."

"You know exactly what it means." Richie pounded the desktop to punctuate his words. He leaned closer to Nolan. "And everyone knows that not a thing happens in a bank without data operations processing it. To the cops, that makes you as complicit as everyone else."

"And," Shay said, "you moved API Holdings account information off the bank's system. You scrubbed it clean. What's that, if not proof that you're involved?"

"Really, guys." Nolan's voice squeaked, and he raised his hands high. "I had nothing to do with this. I only did that because the branch manager insisted. He gave me a bullshit reason, but the guy is my boss."

"How could you not know it was illegal?" Richie asked.

"I didn't know—or want to know—any of the details!" Nolan cried. "But I've got a thumb drive with the account information on it. I'll give it to the police or whoever."

"I'll need to see it first," Shay said, "to make sure it's what you say it is."

"Sure. I'll do whatever I can to help you to prove I'm innocent. Really, I paid no attention to what they processed. For one thing, why would I care? I mean, this API Holdings that you talk about, it didn't mean a thing to me. Really."

Richie looked at Shay. "I suppose, if Nolan here gives us a bit more information to back up what the police and the Feds have against Skarzer and Yamada, they might be willing to see him as someone who is assisting them rather than an accessory to a crime."

"You could be right," Shay said to Richie.

Nolan looked hopeful for the first time. "He *is* right. I can help you. Really. This computer—I can log into the bank's system. Whatever you need, I can find it."

Shay eyed Nolan. "I know exactly what we need to give the Feds, as well as the police, as proof that money laundering was going on here, and that the bank's officers did nothing about it. I'll tell you what we need, you get it for us, and only after that will we make sure that you're off the hook—at least in this API Holding situation."

Nolan swallowed hard, then nodded. He put his hands over the keyboard. "I'll login from here and you tell me what you want."

∽

Mrs. Brannigan had already retired for the night when Shay's doorbell rang. He froze. Someone coming to see him after midnight couldn't possibly be good news. He didn't think it would be Richie. After their little "meeting" with Ethan Nolan, they had worked out a plan. Unless more news broke, Richie didn't need to see him in person. And he didn't think Rebecca had enough evidence to arrest him for aiding Salma. Not yet, anyway.

The doorbell rang again. He was afraid it might be Salma

even though she should be safely in Canada. He had heard from the pilot he'd hired to fly her there that everything had gone smoothly. The Lebanese passport he'd commissioned was waiting for her when she arrived in Toronto, along with a good sum of money, and several burner phones, if needed. Hopefully, she would find it easy to blend in with the ever-growing new immigrant population of the city. But he knew she would miss her children terribly. What if she had changed her mind and came back? He hurried down the stairs and flung open the door.

Salma's father stood on the stoop, his granddaughter at his side. "Zair," Shay whispered, looking from him to the girl.

"Gebran gave her to me. He said he didn't want to raise someone else's child, that his mother had been right about Salma all along, and he felt like a fool having believed her for all these years. Salma told me if that ever happened—she knows Gebran well—that I should bring the girl to you."

"What?" Shay was stunned, both at Zair's words and that Salma would think he could care for a child. "I don't know the first thing about—"

"She's a good girl. She'll be no trouble," Zair said. "I think we should come inside and talk. We are both very tired. Your apartment is up the stairs, right?"

"But..."

Without waiting for Shay's response, Zair led the girl up to the living room. Shay shut the door and followed them.

The girl and Zair waited in the middle of the room, a little pink suitcase on the floor at her side. As Shay walked toward them, he felt as if he were marching through nitroglycerin. What the hell had Salma been thinking?

"Don't worry, Shay," the child said as he neared. He froze at her words. Her face was serious, but she didn't appear frightened, which surprised him because he was. The thought of Zair bringing her to him...

"Mama talked to me on the phone," the girl continued. "She said she had to go away—she didn't want to, and it made her cry. But she told me you're my real father. She said you might seem a little scary to me at first, but you're really a nice man, and you'll be good to me." She stopped and seemed to be waiting for his response.

Shay had to clear his throat before his voice would work. "Good."

"I don't mind staying with you, as long as my grandpa can come and visit me sometime. I'll miss my brother, but Mama said Papa likes him, so he should be okay." Her voice went tiny. "Papa said he doesn't want me. Maybe I shouldn't call him Papa anymore."

Shay swallowed hard as he stared down at the child—his daughter—who had taken the upheaval to her life with such stoicism and had given such a long speech. He raised his eyes to Salma's father. "She's really only eight?"

"Yes," Zair said with a knowing smile as he fixed his gaze pointedly at Shay. "And very smart. Too smart for Gebran to handle, I'm afraid."

Shay had no idea what to do. A big part of him would have loved to order them from his house and go into his bedroom and shut and lock the door. But she looked so small and was trying hard to be brave.

But when she looked up at him again, the bravery seemed to have vanished. "Do you want me to call you Papa?"

He almost smiled at the question, realizing, yes, she was only eight. "You can call me Shay for now."

Hannah nodded. Her big blue eyes looked around the elegant living room, with paintings, sculptures, and knick-knacks that proclaimed, 'No children live here.' "Will I have my own room?" She sounded a bit breathless, as the full implication of her staying there with him was beginning to hit her.

It was bad enough to think about a stoic child with him, but a frightened one was more than he could handle. He squared his shoulders and said loudly, "Zair, we have to talk. I can't just..."

"Yes," Zair said. "You can. We'll work it out with the legal system. Believe me, seeing the two of you together, it will be best for the girl. And, perhaps, for you."

Zair lifted Hannah's suitcase. "Hannah is exhausted. Where can she sleep tonight?"

Shay ran a hand through his blond hair, surprised to find it wasn't standing on end. It should be. "This way," he said, and led them to the guest room. Like the living room, it was far too elaborately furnished for a child. With irony, Shay realized Hannah would be the first 'guest' to ever use it.

She boosted herself up to sit on the high queen-size bed. Even Shay had to smile as he saw that her feet didn't reach the floor. "This is like a bed for a princess," she said, patting the white floral spread.

"And you are our princess," Zair said. "A very tired princess. Now put on your nightgown and get into bed while I talk to Shay. I'll come back and see you in a little while."

The first flash of fear struck the child's face, and Shay's heart went out to her. "Promise?" she asked.

"Yes, sweetheart," Zair said with a nod. "Don't worry. Your mama knows what's best."

Hannah nodded, and Zair shut the door then followed Shay back to the living room.

"Now before I leave you I must tell you," Zair said wearily as he walked over to the sofa and sat, "what really happened on that terrible day, nine years ago."

Shay sat facing him, puzzled by Zair's words. "What do you mean, what really happened?"

Zair shook his head and then looked down at the floor. "I mean, it's all my fault. Everything. What Salma told you nine years ago, it wasn't true. Yussef did come into the shop looking for Salma on that day, but she wasn't there. Only I was."

Shay braced himself. If Salma wasn't there, that changed everything.

"Yussef was furious," Zair said. "He had seen Salma with you, and followed you both to an apartment building. When she left, he tried to follow her, but there was so much traffic and stop lights that he lost her. He went to the house, but she wasn't there, so he came to the dry cleaner's. She wasn't there, either.

"He yelled at me, saying he would tell Gebran, who would divorce her and keep Adam. He said he would see that we were sent back to Lebanon. He even said he hoped Gebran would kill her for the dishonor she brought to him. He said he might have to kill her himself. He was crazy, ranting, and the more he talked, the more worked up he got. I tried to defend her, but that only enraged him and he came after me. He was much stronger and bigger than I, so I pulled out the gun from under the cash register. Just then, Salma opened the door to the shop. Yussef spun toward her, and that was when I fired the gun. He died quickly.

"I told Salma what had happened. At first she tried to deny that she was in love with someone other than Gebran, but she couldn't. I told her I knew she was in love, because I'd seen her happy for the first time since we arrived in the U.S. She said it was true, but she also believed Yussef would be alive if it weren't for her—that I wasn't his killer, she was.

"She believed that if she called you and told you she had shot Yussef because he was attacking her, you would help us make this all go away and I would be safe. She believed you could do anything. And you did. You hid the body."

"You didn't need to lie to me," Shay said. "How could Salma not know that?"

"There was another, more necessary reason for the lie," Zair said. "That same day, Salma went to Fairuz and also told her she had killed Yussef because Yussef had attacked her, sexually—I cannot use the vile word. Fairuz threatened to go to the police and tell them what Salma had done. Salma said, if so, she would allow the police to test her, and prove what Yussef had done. Fairuz then believed her. She had seen the way he had eyed Salma."

Shay could scarcely believe what he was hearing. "You mean, all this time, when I thought Salma ... she was innocent."

"But it changed her," Zair said. "She was sad. Always sad. I worried about her constantly. And I felt guilt. Guilt because, had I been a braver man and had gone to the police, she might have found some way to overcome everything. Even to find happiness. But I was never that brave."

Shay could hardly breathe. Zair wasn't brave and Salma paid the price for his cowardice. "No," he whispered. "If you went to prison, Salma would have blamed herself. If anything, it would have been worse."

"Perhaps you are right. And if so, that helps a little. But then," Zair continued, "after Yussef's body was found, everything became much, much worse."

Shay frowned. "How?"

"The night Gebran went to the nursing home, the last night Fairuz was alive, he told her that Yussef's body had been found. She then asked to talk to Salma, alone. When Salma arrived at the nursing home, Fairuz said she couldn't keep her secret any longer, and that every day—whenever she looked at Hannah—she realized Salma had lied to her, and was especially suspicious of the reason for Yussef's death. She said she was going to tell the police everything, and to make Salma pay, finally, for what she had done to their family.

"Fairuz told her that Gebran would surely throw Hannah out of his house, that the child would go to live in homes with bad children, or with foster parents who took children in just for the money the state gave them. She told Salma all the horrible things they would do to an intelligent, sensitive little girl. Salma was beside herself.

"She waited until after Fairuz's bed check, then just before she left, she put a pillow over her face, holding it until Fairuz's struggles stopped. Then, Salma quickly and quietly left the nursing home. This time, there was no escape. The police, the woman inspector, suspected too much. Salma had to get away." He drew a folded paper from his pocket and placed it on the coffee table. "She always feared such a moment might come, so she wrote out an affidavit and had it notarized back when Hannah was only four months old. It states that you are the girl's father. She gave it to me to keep. I do not know if this will have any status in an American court, but here it is."

Shay lifted the paper and tried to read it, but he couldn't focus on the legal words used, all he could think about was how to contain the rage that built up inside him—a fierce, deadly rage—as he thought of the injustice that had been done to Salma and to him. Worst of all, it had driven Salma to act in a way completely against the nature of the woman he once knew. He couldn't bear what it had done to her, her loss of innocence and pure goodness, even as he realized she had killed to protect their child. More than ever, his heart, his entire being, ached for the woman he loved, for all she had gone through, and for the complete hopelessness she must have felt.

At that moment, he knew she would never come back here, and that he would never see her again.

He didn't dare allow himself think about that now. Perhaps he couldn't think about it, ever. It hurt too much. He forced himself back to the paper Zair had given him, to read its words. It was just as Zair had described. Shay didn't have any idea what standing such a paper might have in court, but if need be, he was willing to try.

"Now that you know what happened, it is time for me to go somewhere as well," Zair said as he stood. "Perhaps, where I go will be nearer, and yet much farther, than where Salma has journeyed."

He sounded suicidal, Shay thought, realizing how devastated Zair had to be by this. "No," he said. "Salma has done everything, given up everything, so that you and her children will be safe. And Hannah will need you more than ever. No suspicion has turned your way. You must continue with your life as usual."

Zair covered his face with his hands. "How am I supposed to do that? How can I—"

"Please, *jido,* don't go away," Hannah stood in the doorway, barefoot and wearing a long nightgown with drawings of Disney princesses, her eyes filled with tears.

Zair jumped to his feet, horrified. "My God, child, did you hear all this?"

She nodded.

"Come over here, then," Shay said to her, holding out his arm, "and tell your old *'jido'* that you need him. That we all will need him."

She ran to her grandfather, and he held her close as they both cried.

As Shay looked at them, he realized his life had completely changed forever. He also realized that not only was he no longer alone, but that he needed help to deal with this situation. He needed someone he could trust implicitly.

He needed help from Richie.

He looked at the time. Two a.m. Richie was probably heading home from work, or already there, exhausted from his long day. Now wouldn't be the time to tell him about the latest developments. He'd have to wait.

∼

Big Caesar's had closed for the night, and Richie knew that if he got into his Porsche, he would again be followed by a black Lexus SUV. He was sick of being tailed, and it was going to come to an end, right here, right now.

Earlier, he had asked a couple of guys he knew to search the streets for the SUV. In a city filled with expensive cars, it was fairly easy to tell which was the right one—it was the one that didn't have license plates, but only those advertising things dealers put on used cars before the actual plates arrive.

If it had had real plates, he would have given the number to Rebecca and had her run the license to learn who the SUV belonged to. But things were never all that easy.

His guys told him where the car was parked. He usually left at closing time, and took the back door to his Porsche, which he kept parked in a private spot behind the nightclub. Tonight, he changed his clothes from his black suit and black bowtie, the usual combo he wore at work, into a light gray sports coat and red tie. Then he slicked his hair straight back using water and gel, and put on a pair of slightly tinted sunglasses. As quickly as he could, he snuck out of the club by using the doors facing the street—the doors the public used. He noticed a couple of people giving him a strange look as he walked out, and he could only hope no one he knew saw him this way.

He went to the spot where the SUV had been located, a block from the nightclub, on the street he always took as he drove toward home.

He crouched behind a car across the street from the SUV and waited. He figured that soon after closing time, whoever was driving the SUV would get into it and wait there until his Porsche drove by, and then follow him again.

Richie didn't have to wait long before he saw Grant Yamada and another fellow jogging up the street to the SUV. Yamada was about to open the driver's door when Richie bounded across the street, grabbed Yamada by the arm, spun him around, and then pushed him back into the Lexus. He gripped

Yamada's lapels and yelled, "What the hell is your game? I've been watching you following me, and I'm sick of it."

Yamada put his hands up as if he were being arrested. "I don't know what the hell you're talking about. Let go of me!"

Just then, the guy who had been with Yamada circled around the SUV to where the two men faced off, but he had a gun in his hand. "Let Yamada go," he demanded.

Richie saw the gun. Fury flashed through him. If that was how these guys wanted to play, so be it. His fingers tightened on Yamada's lapels and only the rush of adrenaline surging through him helped him swing the big man between himself and the gunman. He gave Yamada a forceful shove right into the armed man. The gun went flying.

Richie ran toward it and gave it a kick so it skittered along the street, ending up under a parked car. The gunman looked at the car then back at Richie. He swung his fist at Richie's jaw.

Richie saw the fist coming, ducked, and at the same time charged the now unarmed gunman, hitting him in the stomach and knocking him down. The gunman's head hit the street hard, temporarily stunning him, and giving Richie a chance to sock him in the face, trying to knock him out. But Yamada decided to jump into the fray, pulled Richie off his friend and socked him in the stomach.

Richie lunged after Yamada with both fists. All the rage, frustration, and the sorrow he felt over everything he learned had happened to Isabella because of this man and his cohorts, came out in a barrage of punches. Yamada went down, but Richie didn't stop hitting him until he felt powerful hands grab his arms and lift him off Yamada.

The gunman, he thought, and broke free, raising his fist to continue the fight, when he saw Vito.

"Stop, boss," Vito shouted. "You're going to kill the guy. Let's get the hell out of here."

Richie breathed heavily, blinking away the fog of pure black anger that had swept over him, an anger beyond anything he'd ever felt before, an anger he didn't know he could possess. He looked at Yamada, cowering on the street, leaning back against the SUV and shaking his head slightly as if trying to focus. The other fellow, whoever he was, was gone.

"It was all Skarzer," Yamada whimpered. "He told me to follow you. I don't know anything about it."

"So you just do whatever Skarzer tells you to do?" Richie said with a sneer.

"In this, yes. I'm innocent."

"No, you're not," Richie said. "And if I ever see you near me, Inspector Mayfield, or anyone else that I care about, that'll be it for you. Do you understand what I'm saying?"

Yamada nodded. "But listen to me," his words were mumbled, his voice low, "you might stop me and maybe Skarzer, but this goes a lot farther than us. To people you can't touch or push around. In the end, you'll pay."

Richie seethed, but held himself in check. "Don't count on it fellow. Vito, watch him as he drives away, and then follow him to make sure he goes straight home."

"Sure boss," Vito said. "I can do that, but if he doesn't do what you say, is it okay if I shoot him?"

"With pleasure," Richie said, then grinned. So did Vito.

Yamada crawled into his SUV and drove off so fast his tires scarcely touched the ground. Vito followed in his Dodge Ram. As Richie watched them go, he smoothed his jacket, tugged at the cuffs of his shirt, and despite the bruises and aches he could already feel forming, he walked back to his Porsche with a definite spring in his step.

31

It was early morning when Richie heard someone ringing his doorbell. He was still in bed and he opened one eye to look at the clock. It was only 10 AM. *What in the world?*

He put on his bathrobe, stumbled to the front door, and opened it.

"We've got to talk." Shay pushed past him into the living room.

"Is there a problem with our plan?" Richie asked as he went into the kitchen and made himself a cup of coffee. "I got home late last night. Vito and I caught Grant Yamada following me. The guy all but wet himself."

"The plan is fine," Shay said, eying Richie's bruised face and the slow way he was walking. "If Yamada got the worst of it, I'd hate to see him this morning."

Richie scowled. "My only excuse is, it was two against one."

Shay shook his head. "Anyway, I've set what I could in motion, and the rest is up to you and your 'friends.' I'm here about something else."

"Would you like some coffee or tea?"

"No thanks," Shay said.

Richie returned to the living room, sipping his coffee, and sat on the sofa. Shay took his favorite easy chair. "So, what's going on?" Richie asked.

"Hannah's at my house," Shay said.

"What?"

"You heard me. A perplexed but thrilled Mrs. Brannigan is busy spoiling her as we speak. Her grandfather brought her to me last night. Salma told him that she wanted me to take care of Hannah if anything happened with Gebran, and it has. Gebran's decided Hannah's not his daughter and doesn't want her."

"Damn," Richie murmured. "But I imagine you assumed something like this might happen."

"It's possible to assume all kinds of things, but when you're faced with the reality of them, it's like a kick to the teeth. I'm not sure how to handle it, or even what I should do. All I know is there's a part of me that thinks maybe I should keep her. I need you to tell me honestly, Richie, am I crazy or what?"

"No, not crazy," Richie said. "After all, she is your daughter, and to hear Rebecca tell it, she is much like you."

"Rebecca's seen her?"

"Not only seen her, but talked to her. Hannah seems to have made a great impression."

"Yeah," Shay said with a small, proud smile. "She is an impressive little thing. And brave. When I left her this morning and told her she was going to have to stay with Mrs. Brannigan, she simply nodded and accepted it. I actually was kind of surprised. But then I realized, what do I know about kids? How can I take care of her properly?"

"Actually," Richie said, "even more pertinent than that is what the law says about this. You can't just suddenly keep a kid that no one knows is your child."

"Salma filled out some paperwork, notarized forms

declaring I'm the father and that she gives me legal right of guardianship."

"Sounds like she thought of everything," Richie said. "But if Gebran decides to challenge those forms, from what I understand, since he's Salma's legal husband and was when the child was conceived, he may still have some legal rights those forms might not overcome."

Shay folded his arms. "I know. I've come up with a two-part plan I want to run past you."

Richie nodded. "I should have known."

"The first part takes care of Zair. Hannah adores her grandfather. I plan to meet Gebran and tell him if he tries to do anything to Zair, or tries to take Hannah back, I'll go to the city's Social Services Department and question his suitability as a father to both his children, Adam as well as Hannah. I'll make it clear to him that I can say enough and do enough that they would take Adam away from him. I'm sure Gebran would do whatever it takes to keep Adam with him."

"Well, I suspect that would work," Richie said. "It gives Gebran what he wants, Adam, and gets rid of what he doesn't want, Hannah."

"That's what I'm thinking, too," Shay said. "And the price for all that, allowing Zair to keep his job, isn't a bad one."

"I imagine the second part of your plan has to do with Salma," Richie said. "About Rebecca looking for her, and that you helped a murderer get away."

Shay nodded. "In a couple of weeks, Salma's suicide note will be discovered. It'll admit to her having killed Yussef and Fairuz, and will say that she is so filled with remorse and so unable to live without her children that she killed herself. I'll leave that note somewhere that the authorities will easily connect it to Rebecca's case. I'm thinking Golden Gate Park, near Yussef's burial spot. The note will allow Rebecca to close both her cases."

"And when they can't find Salma's body?" Richie asked.

"Her car will be discovered parked near the Pacific," Shay said. "It's a harsh, dangerous ocean. Not all bodies lost out there are found."

Richie nodded. "That should work. And you know, of course, Rebecca will see through all that in an instant. It has your way of thinking all over it."

"Maybe so, but she'll have no proof." Shay's lips compressed, his shoulders rigid as he held Richie's gaze. "My concern is you, that you're okay with not telling her everything I've told you."

Richie felt his heart twist at his friend's pain, and that Shay could be driven to doubt him. He struggled to appear nonchalant as he shrugged off the words. "Hey, it's not my story to tell. As far as I'm concerned, it's all just hearsay."

"Good." Shay got up and headed for the door, Richie with him.

As they reached it, Richie gave Shay an affectionate pat on the back. "Take care, my friend. Let me know how it goes, and if you need me to do anything to help."

Shay looked momentarily stricken by the open display of friendship, then the slightest hint of a smile crossed his lips as he said simply, "Thanks."

~

That evening, when Rebecca walked into her apartment, she found Richie sitting on the sofa with Spike curled up at his side, the TV on, a beer and a bowl of popcorn on the coffee table in front of him.

"Well," she said, removing gun, holster, and jacket, "somebody looks comfortable.... Oh, my God! What happened to you?"

"It's nothing, and it looks worse than it feels. Sort of." He grinned... slightly. "Come join me." He patted the spot beside him on the sofa. "I was hoping you'd get here before the news came on. Believe me, you'll want to see this. It'll be on in a minute."

She sat beside him, but couldn't possibly look at the TV, not when his face was such a mess. She gripped his shoulders, studying his newfound cuts and bruises. "Seriously, what happened?"

"I showed someone that I didn't like him."

She frowned. "What did you do to him?"

He grinned. "At least you didn't ask who won."

"Richie!"

"He's a little worse for wear, that's all. Vito showed up, so a clear head prevailed. Okay?"

She still looked askance at him, but knew better than to keep harping on the fight. When he was ready to tell her about it, he would. Since a commercial was still running, she said, "By the way, I spoke to my friend at the FBI—"

"Oh yeah, good old Brandon Seymour. What was it you called him? Brand, was it?"

"Bran," she said. "And—"

"Bran. How could I forget? In fact, my mother always eats All-Bran® when she's—"

"Will you stop!" she insisted. "As I was saying, I spoke with Bran, and he's agreed to look into the situation with API Holdings. He'll be able to handle it as long as everything I told him checks out. If it does, he'll make an arrest very quickly."

"Well, bully for him," Richie muttered, eying the TV as if he was actually interested in a Charmin commercial. She knew he had never liked Special Agent Seymour, especially since she once dated him when she unsuccessfully tried to break up with Richie. "I'm glad," Richie continued in his sarcastic tone, "that this isn't a matter of life and death. In fact, the death has already happened. Heaven help us if we had to rely on good ol' 'Bran' to do anything in a speedy manner."

"He isn't that bad," Rebecca began when Richie interrupted.

"Here we go." He sat up straight, the remote pointed at the TV as he turned up the volume.

Rebecca watched in astonishment as the television screen switched to an outside shot of the Marina branch of Superior Savings Bank. A reporter standing in front of it announced that federal officials had shut down the bank as they investigated illegal money laundering transactions that included payoffs to the management of the branch, and potentially to the entire board of the bank. Those arrested were indicted for their activity, which could lead to jail time as well as the confiscation of all assets, personal and private. Photos of Brian Skarzer and Grant Yamada flashed across the screen.

"Incredible," Rebecca said. "How in the world did you manage that?"

"Me?" Richie did his best to look innocent, which was close to impossible for him. "You think I managed to do any of that?" He put an arm around her shoulders, a smugly self-satisfied grin on his bruised and battered face.

She eyed him. "Hmm. I have a sneaking suspicion you and Shay—or Vito, or both—were behind it, especially since Bran had no idea what I was talking about earlier today when I was filling him in on the suspected money laundering. But now the news is saying that the Feds were involved."

"Actually, I suspect Treasury Department agents led the operation." Now Richie's smile was as broad as she had ever seen it. "And I may happen to know a few guys who work in the San Francisco office."

"Very clever, Mr. Amalfi." Rebecca smiled at him, thankful that this time at least, he not only had stayed within the boundaries of the law, but had worked with the law. Maybe there was hope for him yet, she thought with an inward smile. Except for his fighting. She was also glad that she, too, had managed to stay within the law in this case—except for one little white lie about working on a "cold case" when she asked Deputy Rachel Swann to give her access to Cory Egerton. But all in all, she felt, it was the most minor of infractions. And she'd only been yelled at a couple of times by Lt. Eastwood. Life was good. "It sounds like people will pay for their wrong-doing and greed."

"That's what I hope," Richie said. "At least, I have answers now, not complete answers, but I can live with that. But keep in mind, it wasn't the bankers who left warning notes for you, or who tried to broadside you with a truck, or pulled a gun on you after rear-ending your SUV. Yamada made a threat last night—"

"Ah, so that's who you were tussling with—"

"As I was saying, Yamada warned that there are bigger fish out there. Actually, they're more like sharks—sharks that we can't reach or touch. He said they won't give up. It makes me think they're afraid that we might know too much, which means we're both in danger." His fingers gently touched the side of her face, her hair, her jaw. "I don't want you to be. I want this to be my fight, alone, and for you to be safe."

She angled her head slightly so that the warmth of his palm rested against her cheek. "It's my fight, too. I'm the one who traced the activities to someone, potentially, in City Hall. Whoever is behind this isn't about to forget that. And there's nothing you or I can do about it, but to see that the person behind this monster money laundering scheme—and whatever else is being done to corrupt City Hall—is sent to prison. That's the only way we can *both* be safe again."

"What if the scheme is too big, the players too dangerous?" His gaze was filled with worry, but she knew it was for her, not for himself.

"You know as well as I do, there's no backing out now. We

can't 'unknow' what we've discovered, and because of that, we'll remain in jeopardy until we capture whoever's behind it."

He nodded, knowing she was right.

"The good news, for the moment at least," she continued, "is that all has been quiet along that front for some time."

"They might have been scared off by Vito," Richie said, then frowned. "Wait, though. Vito never did explain how he ended up at Big Caesar's last night to help me when he was supposed to be watching you."

Her eyebrows rose. "Maybe I knew he was watching me, so when I decided to retire for the night, I told him I was locking up my apartment and sleeping with my Glock under my pillow. That way, he would rest easy and go home—or wherever he thought he might be more needed."

He looked skeptical. "Maybe so."

"Well, whatever might be going on, I'm sure we'll figure it out. Everything will turn out fine."

"I'm working on it," Richie admitted.

That was a strange thing for him to say. "What do you mean?"

He looked guilty. "Nothing. I don't mean a thing." As quickly as it hit, the guilt vanished as he said, "I almost forgot to tell you about Shay. His daughter is with him."

"She is?" Rebecca was stunned.

Richie quickly told her about Hannah's plight and Shay's reaction. "My God, Rebecca. We're going to have to keep a suicide watch on him as he tries to figure out how to deal with having a daughter. He'll have to learn to associate with all kinds of people, and God help us, pretend to be friendly to them."

"Still, it sounds like he's doing the right thing," she said. "He wants to keep her and give her a good home, despite everything that happened between him and Salma."

"That's for sure." Richie nodded. "He only met her yesterday, but from what I've seen, heaven help anyone who tries to step between them."

"Good. I'm so glad." She was smiling, and so was Richie. But as she looked at him, tears filled her eyes. She did her best to blink them away so he wouldn't notice. The ironic part was that they weren't tears of sadness, but of happiness. She felt good that these two men that she had somehow learned to care about, and even—yes, she admitted—to love, suddenly had a lot of answers that they'd spent years looking for. She loved it when that happened, but hated it when she turned all sappy.

"Hey, what's this?" Richie studied her face.

"Nothing," she said, but then admitted, "Sometimes even hardened cops get a little sentimental. Things might not be perfect, but whatever is? Still, I'm happy that you both have more answers now than you did a short while ago. And for Shay, I can only hope that somehow things will work out." She bowed her head, not wanting to even think about what the future might bring to her case. "I'd hate to have to arrest Salma. That would be tough."

"Don't worry," Richie said. "I'm sure everything will be fine, uh, so to speak."

Something about his words definitely made her suspicious, but right now, she didn't care. "I hope you're right, Richie, I truly do."

"When am I ever wrong?"

"You are so egotistical," she said with a laugh, then turned toward him and stroked his hair back. "You're going to have a nice shiner to go with all the cuts and other bruises, I'm afraid. But even when you've been beaten up, you're still too handsome by half."

He caught her hands in his, then gazed at her, his brows slightly crossed.

"What is it?" she asked.

"You. I was just thinking of all you mean to me. Of how

much you've come to mean to me in such a surprisingly short time."

His words surprised her. "That's funny. Not long ago, I was thinking the exact same thing about you, and wondering ..."

"Wondering?" he asked.

Here I go again, she thought, ready to blow up a good thing. "As I was reading the reports ... about Isabella's accident and all, and how much you loved her, I couldn't help but..." She couldn't go on.

His hands tightened on hers. "Isabella will always be in my heart, Rebecca. She was a wonderful person." And then, his voice broke ever so slightly as he whispered the next words to her. "But I believe my heart is big enough to have room for more than one person in it. I hope you believe that as well."

With that, he let go of her as if to say it was her choice to make.

She remained absolutely still for a few seconds, her blue eyes capturing his deep, dark brown ones, as his few simple words filled her and broke through the carefully constructed barrier she used as a shield. Her heart opened to him completely. She loved him. She knew it by the beat her heart skipped whenever he came into view, by the little surge she felt when he gazed at her with tenderness, by her trust in him. Love was opening the door to her apartment and finding him there patiently waiting for her, a scruffy little dog on his lap. Love was the heat she felt on her face when he was close to her, and the quickening deep inside when he moved even closer. It was physical, it was mental, it was all-consuming. It was scary.

"I've watched your friends and family react to you," she murmured, her palm lightly caressing the side of his face. "They know you well, and they love and trust you completely. How could I not believe you? How could I not feel the same way?"

He shifted so that he was sitting up in front of her while she remained against the sofa's back cushions. The way he looked at her, she knew what he was feeling, but she could tell he was also struggling to somehow ease the emotions that flowed between them. "My offer for you to move in with me still stands," he said lightly, but almost immediately, the lightness vanished. "It'll always stand."

"You're sure?" she whispered.

"Yes, and I've been sure for a long, long time. It's you," he said, his voice husky and heartfelt as he leaned closer. "Only you." And then he kissed her.

PLUS ...

Find out what happens next in the lives of Rebecca and Richie when the clock strikes **SEVEN O'CLOCK.** To hear about the next Rebecca and Richie story, and all of Joanne's new books, please sign up for her **New Release Mailing List.**

∽

In the meantime, while waiting for "Seven O'Clock," you might be interested in learning more about Richie's cousin, Angie Amalfi, and her fiance, Rebecca's fellow homicide detective, Paavo Smith.

Their stories are a mixture of culinary and "ghostly" situations. The first mystery in their new series is *COOKING SPIRITS: An Angie & Friends Food & Spirits Mystery,* in which "culinary queen" Angie Amalfi puts aside her gourmet utensils to concentrate on planning her upcoming wedding to Paavo. But instead of the answer to her heart's dreams, she scrambles to deal with wedding planners with bizarre ideas, wedding dresses that don't flatter, squabbling relatives with hurt feelings, a long-suffering groom, and worries over where she and Paavo will live after the wedding. Soon, all of that pales when Angie finds the perfect house for them, except for one little problem ... the house may be haunted.

For your enjoyment, here's Chapter 1 of *Cooking Spirits*:

Not much remained to identify.

San Francisco Homicide Inspector Paavo Smith and his partner, Toshiro Yoshiwara, stood in an alley in the city's Financial District surrounded by high-rise offices with restaurants, delis, bars, and a myriad of shops filling the ground floors. The alley mainly existed for garbage pickup.

They had seen many dead bodies in their time, but none as mangled as the poor sap before them. The brightness of the morning sun, the beauty of a new day, seemed bizarrely at odds with watching the medical examiner's team pull body parts, piece by piece, from a garbage truck. Even hardened crime scene investigators struggled to keep their breakfasts down.

Earlier, one of the scavengers on the route had been wheeling a dumpster back into place when his partner operating the truck told him to climb up to see why the trash compactor seemed to be straining. The scavenger saw the human legs and feet—jeans and a man's leather slip-ons—slowly being sucked into the mechanism. He screamed for his partner to cut the power, but it was too late. Only one foot had been saved.

Blood dampened the ground in front of the location where the dumpster had been, making it appear as if an altercation had taken place there. The victim must have been tossed into the dumpster.

"We won't be able to tell anything until the medical examiner's team sorts all this out," Paavo said, although from the color, hardness and lividity of the foot that hadn't been smashed, the death may have occurred a day or so earlier. He tried to find a jacket or pants pockets to look for a wallet or other identifying papers, but at the moment neither pockets nor their contents were identifiable. Finally, he peered with dismay at their crime scene.

They stood in the busiest section of San Francisco during the week, and one of the quietest areas on weekends. The job of canvassing the Financial District and talking to anyone who might have seen or heard something would be a nightmare.

"The poor bastard's teeth were crushed when his head went through the compactor," Yosh said. "Dental records won't help."

Paavo nodded. "Let's hope we have some fingerprints on file."

"Yeah," Yosh said, "once we find his fingers."

∽

Angelina Amalfi had just entered her penthouse apartment high atop San Francisco's Russian Hill when she heard a knock on her door.

"I was just thinking about you, Angie," her across-the-hall neighbor, Stanfield Bonnette, said as he strolled in. "And then I heard your door. You look tired."

"I am tired." She tossed her jacket over the arm of a chair, kicked off her four-inch high heels, and plopped herself down on the sofa.

Stan sat beside her. He was thirty, thin and wiry with light brown hair and brown eyes.

His was the only other apartment on the top floor of the twelve-story building on the corner of Green and Vallejo Streets. Stan could afford his place thanks to his father, a bank executive. And thanks to him, Stan had a job at the bank. His father's help didn't motivate Stan to work hard—or to work at all for that matter.

"I just fired the worst wedding planner the world has ever known," Angie said wearily.

His eyebrows rose high. "You fired her? I thought you needed someone to help you with your wedding."

"I do. That's the problem." She leaned forward and rubbed her temples. "But she kept pushing a wedding dress cut too low with a bouffant skirt that puffed out at the waist. I'm short. I've been clothing this short body for many years. I know that with so little material on top, and so much on the bottom I'd look like a marshmallow. And I did. She insisted the dress was perfect, and I 'needed' to buy it without letting my mother or sister or anyone else give an opinion. She said families only confused the bride."

"That may be true." Stan shuddered at the mention of Angie's mother and sisters.

"As if that wasn't bad enough, she wanted the reception to be decorated in blue. I'm not a blue person. I'm Italian!" She heaved a sigh. "Finally, I realized the only thing I 'needed' was a new wedding planner. One not so bossy."

She picked up a See's chocolate from the candy dish on the coffee table and took a bite, chewing morosely. Raspberry cream. She didn't even like raspberry cream, but ate it anyway. She was truly miserable. Wedding planning was a stress test, and she was losing.

Stan had wandered off to the kitchen as Angie talked. "Tell you what." His voice sounded muffled as he perused left-overs in the refrigerator. "Why don't I help you cook dinner tonight? After we eat, you'll feel a lot better, I'm sure."

Despite his words, Stan couldn't cook. "Eat whatever you'd like, Stan. Paavo's coming over later, and we're going out to dinner." She took another chocolate, this one a caramel chew, as she thought about her handsome fiancé. She loved everything about his looks from his thick, dark brown hair, to his high forehead, penetrating light blue eyes, high cheekbones, and aquiline nose with a small jog in the middle where it had been broken. He was broad-shouldered, his body long and lean, and everything about him exuded power and, to her, more sexiness than one man should possess.

The whirring of her microwave pulled her from her daydreams.

Stan put a placemat on the dining room table and in another minute carried a dish with two pieces of Chicken Kiev. "I tell you, Angie, if you were marrying me, I'd be home every night for dinner."

"I know." One of the ironies of her relationship with Paavo was that his busy schedule often caused him to work late into the night and miss dinner. At the moment, he had no complicated cases that she knew of, which meant he should have time to help with their wedding plans. "I hope, once we're married and living together, we'll share more meals. That reminds me, I've got to clear out some of my things so he'll have room here."

"Oh my God!" Stan put down his fork before he'd finished, a remarkable thing for him. "You aren't saying he's moving into this apartment, are you?"

"Of course he is. I can't fit into his house. It has only one bedroom, one bathroom. Not even a dining room."

"Angie, you can't expect him to live in your father's apartment building!" Stan said, digging in again with gusto to make up for lost time.

Angie had already recognized that it wasn't a stellar idea, but she hated hearing Stan say it. "My father might own the building, but we've always considered this to be my apartment. I'll clean out the den and make it Paavo's 'man cave.' He'll like that."

Stan took another bite, savoring the rich flavors as he digested the information. "But if you do that, where will you put your desk and computer and all your business books?"

"For all the good they've done me!" Angie interrupted. Now,

she was not only tired, but dejected as well. Her inability to create a rewarding career for herself was one of the banes of her life. She had a talent for cooking, but even though she had tried to become a cake baker, a candy maker, newspaper food columnist, restaurant reviewer, took part in a radio cooking show *and* a TV cooking show, and on and on... nothing ever worked out.

Stan frowned as he savored the last bite of Chicken Kiev. "Paavo living here is not going to work, Angie. If I were him, I'd hate living in your apartment. In fact, I'd do everything I could to postpone the wedding just to avoid it. Just wait. He's going to back out of this. First, he'll start breaking dates with you. Next, he'll suggest the wedding be postponed. You'll see."

"Paavo wouldn't do that," she said, glaring fiercely.

He sniffed. "Paavo doesn't want to upset you so he'll suffer in silence, growing more and more unhappy every day until, finally, he'll walk out on you."

"Nonsense! That's a horrible thing to say." But even as she protested, she knew Paavo held things inside if troubled. He would turn quiet and distant instead of blathering and complaining the way she did. When she first met him, she thought he was cold because of that. Quickly, she learned how much he felt—sometimes too much.

Stan put his plate, fork and knife in the dishwasher. "He'll deny it, but that doesn't mean he'll like being here."

Angie fumed. How could he know more about Paavo than she did? And yet, Paavo never actually said he wanted to move into her apartment, just that he agreed she couldn't fit all her stuff into his little house. "I'm busy, Stan. Why don't you go home?"

He poured himself a generous glass of the Beringer Petite Sirah. "You can kick me out, but that doesn't mean you should ignore my advice." Holding the wine, he headed out the door.

She folded her arms and sat back on the sofa, but she couldn't stop the question reverberating in her head: *What if Stan was right?*

Continue with COOKING SPIRITS: An Angie & Friends Food & Spirits Mystery wherever fine books and ebooks are sold.

ABOUT THE AUTHOR

Joanne Pence was born and raised in northern California. She has been an award-winning, *USA Today* best-selling author of mysteries for many years, but she has also written historical fiction, contemporary romance, romantic suspense, a fantasy, and supernatural suspense. All of her books are now available as ebooks and in print, and many are also offered in special large print editions. Joanne hopes you'll enjoy her books, which present a variety of times, places, and reading experiences, from mysterious to thrilling, emotional to lightly humorous, as well as powerful tales of times long past.

Visit her at www.joannepence.com and be sure to sign up for Joanne's mailing list to hear about new books.

The Rebecca Mayfield Mysteries

Rebecca is a by-the-book detective, who walks the straight and narrow in her work, and in her life. Richie, on the other hand, is not at all by-the-book. But opposites can and do attract, and there are few mystery two-somes quite as opposite as Rebecca and Richie.

ONE O'CLOCK HUSTLE – North American Book Award winner in Mystery
TWO O'CLOCK HEIST
THREE O'CLOCK SÉANCE
FOUR O'CLOCK SIZZLE
FIVE O'CLOCK TWIST

SIX O'CLOCK SILENCE
Plus a Christmas Novella: The Thirteenth Santa

The Angie & Friends Food & Spirits Mysteries

Angie Amalfi and Homicide Inspector Paavo Smith are soon to be married in this latest mystery series. Crime and calories plus a new "twist" in Angie's life in the form of a ghostly family inhabiting the house she and Paavo buy, create a mystery series with a "spirited" sense of fun and adventure.

COOKING SPIRITS
ADD A PINCH OF MURDER
COOK'S BIG DAY
MURDER BY DEVIL'S FOOD
Plus a Christmas mystery-fantasy: COOK'S CURIOUS CHRISTMAS
And a cookbook: COOK'S DESSERT COOKBOOK

The early "Angie Amalfi mystery series" began when Angie first met San Francisco Homicide Inspector Paavo Smith. Here are those mysteries in the order written:

SOMETHING'S COOKING
TOO MANY COOKS
COOKING UP TROUBLE
COOKING MOST DEADLY
COOK'S NIGHT OUT
COOKS OVERBOARD
A COOK IN TIME
TO CATCH A COOK
BELL, COOK, AND CANDLE
IF COOKS COULD KILL
TWO COOKS A-KILLING
COURTING DISASTER
RED HOT MURDER

THE DA VINCI COOK

Supernatural Suspense

Ancient Echoes
Top Idaho Fiction Book Award Winner
Over two hundred years ago, a covert expedition shadowing Lewis and Clark disappeared in the wilderness of Central Idaho. Now, seven anthropology students and their professor vanish in the same area. The key to finding them lies in an ancient secret, one that men throughout history have sought to unveil.

Michael Rempart is a brilliant archeologist with a colorful and controversial career, but he is plagued by a sense of the supernatural and a spiritual intuitiveness. Joining Michael are a CIA consultant on paranormal phenomena, a washed-up local sheriff, and a former scholar of Egyptology. All must overcome their personal demons as they attempt to save the students and learn the expedition's terrible secret....

Ancient Shadows
One by one, a horror film director, a judge, and a newspaper publisher meet brutal deaths. A link exists between them, and the deaths have only begun ....
Archeologist Michael Rempart finds himself pitted against ancient demons and modern conspirators when a dying priest gives him a powerful artifact—a pearl said to have granted Genghis Khan the power, eight centuries ago, to lead his Mongol warriors across the steppes to the gates of Vienna.

The artifact has set off centuries of war and destruction as it conjures demons to play upon men's strongest ambitions and cruelest desires. Michael realizes the so-called pearl is a philosopher's stone, the prime agent of alchemy. As much as he would like to ignore the artifact, when he sees horrific deaths and experiences, first-hand, diabolical possession and affliction, he has no choice but to act, to follow a path along the Old Silk Road to a land that time forgot, and to somehow find a place that may no longer exist in the world as he knows it.

Ancient Illusions

A long-lost diary, a rare book of ghost stories, and unrelenting nightmares combine to send archeologist Michael Rempart on a forbidden journey into the occult and his own past.

When Michael returns to his family home after more than a decade-long absence, he is rocked by the emotion and intensity of the memories it awakens. His father is reclusive, secretive, and obsessed with alchemy and its secrets—secrets that Michael possesses. He believes the way to end this sudden onslaught of nightmares is to confront his disturbing past.

But he soon learns he isn't the only one under attack. Others in his life are also being tormented by demonic nightmares that turn into a deadly reality. Forces from this world and other realms promise madness and death unless they obtain the powerful, ancient secrets in Michael's possession. Their violence creates an urgency Michael cannot ignore. The key to defeating them seems to lie in a land of dreams inhabited by ghosts ... and demons.

From the windswept shores of Cape Cod to a mystical land where samurai and daimyo once walked, Michael must find a way to stop not only the demons, but his own father. Yet, doing so, he fears may unleash an ancient evil upon the world that he will be powerless to contain.

Historical, Contemporary & Fantasy Romance

Dance with a Gunfighter

Gabriella Devere wants vengeance. She grows up quickly when she witnesses the murder of her family by a gang of outlaws, and vows to make them pay for their crime. When the law won't help her, she takes matters into her own hands.

Jess McLowry left his war-torn Southern home to head West, where he hired out his gun. When he learns what happened to Gabriella's family, and what she plans, he knows a young woman like her will have no chance against the outlaws, and vows to save her the way he couldn't save his own family.

But the price of vengeance is high and Gabriella's willingness to sacrifice everything ultimately leads to the book's deadly and startling conclusion.

Willa Cather Literary Award finalist for Best Historical Novel.

The Dragon's Lady

Turn-of-the-century San Francisco comes to life in this romance of star-crossed lovers whose love is forbidden by both society and the laws of the time.

Ruth Greer, wealthy daughter of a shipping magnate, finds a young boy who has run away from his home in Chinatown—an area of gambling parlors, opium dens, and sing-song girls, as well as families trying to eke out a living. It is also home to the infamous and deadly "hatchet men" of Chinese lore.

There, Ruth meets Li Han-lin, a handsome, enigmatic leader of one such tong, and discovers he is neither as frightening cruel, or wanton as reputation would have her believe. As Ruth's fascination with the lawless area grows, she finds herself pulled deeper into its intrigue and dangers, particularly those surrounding Han-lin. But the two are from completely different worlds, and when both worlds are shattered by the Great Earthquake and Fire of 1906 that destroyed most of San Francisco, they face their ultimate test.

Seems Like Old Times

When Lee Reynolds, nationally known television news anchor, returns to the small town where she was born to sell her now-vacant childhood home, little does she expect to find that her first love has moved back to town. Nor does she expect that her feelings for him are still so strong.

Tony Santos had been a major league baseball player, but now finds his days of glory gone. He's gone back home to raise his young son as a single dad.

Both Tony and Lee have changed a lot. Yet, being with him, she finds that in her heart, it seems like old times...

The Ghost of Squire House

For decades, the home built by reclusive artist, Paul Squire, has stood empty on a windswept cliff overlooking the ocean. Those who attempted to live in the home soon fled in terror. Jennifer Barrett knows nothing of the history of the house she inherited. All she knows is she's glad for the chance to make a new life for herself.

It's Paul Squire's duty to rid his home of intruders, but something about this latest newcomer's vulnerable status ... and resemblance of someone from his past ... dulls his resolve. Jennifer would like to find a real flesh-and-blood man to liven her days and nights—someone to share her life with—but living in the artist's house, studying his paintings, she is surprised at how close she feels to him.

A compelling, prickly ghost with a tortured, guilt-ridden past, and a lonely heroine determined to start fresh, find themselves in a battle of wills and emotion in this ghostly fantasy of love, time, and chance.

Dangerous Journey

C.J. Perkins is trying to find her brother who went missing while on a Peace Corps assignment in Asia. All she knows is that the disappearance has something to do with a "White Dragon." Darius Kane, adventurer and bounty hunter, seems to be her only hope, and she practically shanghais him into helping her.

With a touch of the romantic adventure film Romancing the Stone, C.J. and Darius follow a trail that takes them through the narrow streets of Hong Kong, the backrooms of San Francisco's Chinatown, and the wild jungles of Borneo as they pursue both her brother and the White Dragon. The closer C.J. gets to them, the more danger she finds herself in—and it's not just danger of losing her life, but also of losing her heart.

Made in United States
Troutdale, OR
04/13/2024